THE N

He sudd ... to Thornb ... ow your guts out,'' he hissed venomously.

Thornberry gasped, and the cigarette in his hand described a swift arc downward.

"Hondo Horn!'' he burst out involuntarily.

"Get 'em up, and keep shut,'' Hondo whispered viciously.

The man's hands started up, the right one still holding the cigarette. But suddenly he jabbed the lighted end of the cigarette straight into Hondo's face and struck viciously at the gun pressed against his stomach with the other . . .

Available in Fontana by the same author

Man Bait
Rope Crazy
Saddle on a Cloud
Windy Jake's Legacy

FRANK C. ROBERTSON

The Noose Hangs High

FONTANA / Collins

First published in 1944 by William Collins Sons & Co Ltd
First issued in Fontana Books 1965
Second Impression May 1975

Made and printed in Great Britain by
William Collins Sons & Co Ltd Glasgow

CONTENTS

DAPHNE DIXON clutched her skirt with one hand and grabbed at her hat with the other as the rear end of the train passed, exposing her to the vicious teeth of a thirty-mile gale. At the other end of the depot platform her two canvas valises lay forlornly where the baggage smashers had tossed them. It was cold. The sun, scarce half an hour up, was but a red blur against the dust. Her eyes rested upon a faded and battered sign across a rutty roadway.

ESMERALDA

GEM OF THE WEST

The locomotive wailed for a crossing, and a dismal silence settled over the town. Daphne advanced resolutely into the waiting-room and spoke to the aged operator.

"Can you tell me when the stage leaves here for Highline?"

"Two o'clock, miss. It can't go till it gits in. Used to be the stage left here in the mornin', an' come back at night. Then Highline got so proud as Esmeralder began to fold up that the stage leaves there in the mornin' an' gits back at night. But don't blame me. Blame old George A. Kump if you have to blame anybody. When he moved his bank up there he jest naturally sounded the death-knell for Esmeralder."

"That's too bad," Daphne said. Under other circumstances she would have been amused by the garrulous old telegrapher, but now her mind was weighed by trouble. Bad trouble.

"Stage station is in the Commercial Hotel yonder, but if them bags of your'n are heavy you can leave 'em in here an' have Dave Skinner pick 'em up before he starts back with the stage."

"Thank you, I'll just carry them over myself," Daphne said. "They're not heavy."

"Suit yourself," the operator said, and began tapping out a message.

Daphne picked up a valise in each hand and started across

the street in the face of the gale. Her hat blew to the back of her head, but was anchored there by a long hat-pin through her mass of soft brown hair. Her skirts whipped at her knees, and she had to battle them down with the two valises.

She pulled up in the grateful shelter of a large, square wooden hotel feeling as if she had just swum a river, except that she was still dry. She had to gasp desperately in the sudden vacuum to get back her breath. Then she marched into the small lobby of the hotel.

A counter across one end of the room bore a pasteboard placard,

HIGHLINE STAGE

The room was empty. Daphne carried her bags over to the counter and set them down. She went back to the desk and contemplated ringing the silver desk bell, but with her hand poised above it she saw a woman coming down the stairs.

The woman was dressed in black and carried a heavy coat and a man's hat over her arm. She was young, probably twenty-five, with fresh red cheeks and smooth black hair braided and bundled at the back of her neck. A plain woman, a little on the dowdy side, but good-natured and intelligent, Daphne thought with a woman's swift appraisal of another woman. When the woman reached the foot of the stairs Daphne saw that she also carried thick leather gloves, and wore strong, serviceable shoes.

"Hello," the woman greeted cheerily. "You look pretty well froze up. Just come in on that train?"

"Yes," Daphne replied, trying to keep her teeth from chattering. "It was warm on the train, and this wind——"

"You can't tell me a thing about an Esmeralda wind," the woman laughed. "What you need is a hot cup of coffee and some breakfast. Come on, we'll go back and put that lazy Chink to work."

Daphne warmed to the woman instantly. Despite the dread in her soul she smiled, and her companion said, "You're awfully pretty. What in the world are you doing in Esmeralda?"

"I am going to Highline when the stage leaves," Daphne replied.

"So? What's your name, honey? I'm Bessie Bell."

"I'm Daphne Dixon."

Bessie's plump, somewhat calloused hand had been half extended when she introduced herself, but she withdrew it suddenly as though she had been about to touch something hot. The smile on her face froze for a second, then evaporated.

"Well, now we know each other," she said, and gave a short, brittle laugh. "Come on."

Bessie led the way into a long, vacant dining room.

"Hop Sing," she called out. "Where are you, you slant-eyed son of the Orient?"

A grinning yellow face appeared at the window counter connecting dining room with kitchen. "Me here, Mliss Blessie. You likee blekfast?"

"For two. And chop-chop," Bessie replied.

"Chop-chop—light away," the Chinaman said.

"Just as well sit down here," Bessie said. "Better take your coat off so you'll feel it when you go out. And your hat is cock-eyed."

Daphne dutifully removed her hat and coat, and sat down miserably. She was hurt by the abrupt change in manner of her companion, but she told herself that was something she had to get used to. But she was resentful, and knew that her temper was likely to explode at any moment.

They were silent for a few minutes; Daphne absolutely motionless, Bessie tapping the table gently with her fingers.

"You Willard Dixon's sister?" Bessie asked abruptly.

"Yes. You know him?" Daphne asked challengingly.

"I know him. I thought he was a nice boy——for a while."

"What right have you to say he isn't?" Daphne demanded fiercely. "He hasn't been convicted of anything yet, has he?"

"No, he hasn't," Bessie said quietly.

"Then what right have you to judge him before a trial?"

"Probably the best right in the world," Bessie answered surprisingly. "But let's go back a ways—back to where I started in being rude. Will you shake hands now? I've got nothing on earth against *you*."

Daphne hesitated. This woman had refused to shake hands with her, and she had the same right of refusal. But somehow, there was a look of such rugged honesty on Bessie's plain features that she found it hard to resist. Slowly she passed her hand across the table. Bessie gave it a warm pressure.

"I always hate to be caught with my—by surprise," Bessie said. "That's the way you got me a minute ago. Now maybe we'll be able to get along better. You see, I live in Highline."

"And you think my brother is a thief?" Daphne commented.

"I don't know," Bessie replied. "Honestly, I don't know whether he is a thief or not. But I do know that he is trying to crawl out of his jam by putting the blame on a man that I know is innocent, a man who could have my right arm any time he wanted to ask for it. Right arm, hell! he could have all of me. Any time, any place."

Daphne felt herself moved. She had been right about this woman's forthright honesty.

"You love this man—whoever he is—I take it," she said.

"To keep his feet dry I'd lay down in the mud and let him walk on me."

"I never loved a man," Daphne said slowly. "If I ever do I suppose it will be like that."

"For your sake I hope not," Bessie sighed. "Especially if you're the wrong woman for the right man." Bessie looked away for a moment. Then she said, "There's no use for you to wait for the stage. I'm driving out in about an hour and you had just as well ride with me."

"Maybe we'd better get some things straight first," Daphne said. "Why do you hate my brother?"

"All right. What do you know about his case?"

"Very little," Daphne admitted. "Willard would have died before he'd tell me he was in trouble. Fortunately, his lawyer, a Mr. Abel, found my address and wrote me. But all he said was that Willard had been accused of stealing cattle."

"And Abel said he would be convicted if you didn't dig up some money."

"I haven't got very much—about five hundred dollars I've saved. I work in a bank. But I came right out to see what I could do. I know Willard has been wild, but he isn't a thief. I know that." She finished with convincing emphasis, and Bessie nodded slowly.

"You don't know any details then?" Bessie asked.

"None."

"This is what happened. Last summer your brother rode for the K Bar K outfit. It belongs to George A. Kump, cattleman and banker whom everybody calls George A. He's a fine old man even if he is rich.

"Well, honey, Willard's only fault seemed to be that he was

a fool to gamble. He could have stayed on all winter. I happen to know that the foreman liked him. But he quit. Said he had got a better job. He disappeared for a while.

"Along toward spring a trapper drifted into an isolated hay ranch away back in the mountains, and he found Willard feeding a bunch of cattle there. They were K Bar K cows, and Willard told the trapper he was feeding them for George A."

"Well, wasn't he?" Daphne demanded.

"It happened he wasn't. This trapper happened to mention it to Hondo Horn, the K Bar K foreman, but he didn't know what the name of the feeder was. Hondo at once got the sheriff and they rode out there. The cattle had been stolen. It was a bunch that had been held back in the hills when the winter round-up was on.

"I guess your brother was pretty scared, and to save himself he insisted that Hondo Horn himself had hired him to feed the cattle. More than that he claimed Hondo had given him cash to buy the hay from the rancher."

"If Willard said that, then I believe him," Daphne said spiritedly.

"And I," Bessie stated quietly, "know that he lied."

"How do you know? How *can* you know?" Daphne demanded.

"Because Hondo Horn is that man I was talkin' about. He wouldn't steal, and he wouldn't lie—even to save himself. But here comes our Celestial friend with our breakfast. You've got a long, cold ride ahead of you so you'll need to stow a lot of grub under your belt."

CHAPTER II — DAPHNE BITES THE DUST

WHAT she had just heard had taken away Daphne's appetite, but it came back with a rush when she started to eat. She was young and healthy, and hungry. After all it didn't sound as bad as she had expected. Bessie Bell was plainly a prejudiced witness, and it seemed to boil down to a question of veracity. Why shouldn't a jury believe Willard as well as this Hondo Horn? Of course if Bessie loved the man as much as she said—and Daphne couldn't doubt it—then it was natural for Bessie to believe Horn, just as it was natural for her to believe Willard.

The subject had been dropped by tacit agreement. Daphne would have been completely confident of Willard's innocence except for one small atom of doubt.

She was two years older than Willard, and most unwillingly she could remember instances when he, caught in some boyish jam, had cravenly tried to lie himself out of it by putting the blame on other people. But that had been long ago, and any boy might have done the same. He was grown up now, almost twenty-one. He wouldn't try to lie an innocent man into the penitentiary to save himself if he was guilty.

And one thing she did know. With all his faults Willard had never been a thief.

By the time the meal was finished Daphne was actually feeling sorry for her companion, although Bessie was the sort of person, she realized, who would scorn pity, or even sympathy.

"You stick around in the lobby where it's warm till I call for you," Bessie said when they had finished. "I won't be much over an hour." She would have paid for Daphne's meal only the girl refused to let her.

"I do appreciate you giving me a ride, Miss Bell," Daphne said. "Especially under the circumstances."

"Forget it. And it's not Miss Bell, it's Mrs. Only my friends all call me Bessie. I hope I'll be Bessie to you, too."

"Thank you."

"I happen to be a widow," Bessie turned back to say.

During the next twenty minutes a busy little woman who seemed to be landlady passed through the lobby several times. She gave Daphne a smiling nod, and paid her no more attention. One or two men looked inside. Some went through to the dining room, and a few withdrew to the street.

Finally a big man, with a sheepskin collar on his duck coat turned up around his ears, entered the room. His eyes reminded Daphne of the yellow-specked agate marbles which her brother had owned as a boy. There seemed to be no expression in them, yet they were illuminated by a remote light that touched upon the object of his vision like the cold feel of pieces of steel. His eyes flicked over the room and rested upon Daphne. His lids seemed to half close, while the lips of an almost abnormally small mouth opened slightly.

"I'm looking for my little sweetheart, Bessie Bell. Yon seen anything of her?" he asked suddenly in a high, almost piping voice.

"She left here a little while ago, but she said she would be back soon," Daphne answered civilly.

"Oh, she did, eh? Say, who are you? I never seen you before."

"I think we're even."

"Hunh? Well, you don't need to git huffy. If you're goin' to be around here long you might see a lot of me." He turned and went out.

Hondo Horn. So that was the fellow Bessie was in love with, the man she would believe over Willard? He was just such a man as she had pictured from the moment Bessie had mentioned him.

She had no doubt in the world that this was Hondo Horn.

It was still another hour before Bessie appeared. She was driving a trim pair of little brown mares to a single-seated, black-topped Spaulding buggy. She shouted loudly, "Hey, Daphne!"

Daphne stepped quickly to the door.

"Bring your grips and stuff 'em under the lid in the back," Bessie directed. "I've got to hold my horses."

Daphne got the two valises, but a man coming out of the dining room took them out of her hands and placed them in the back of the buggy.

"Hi, yuh, Bess," the man said. "How's business?"

"Couldn't be better, Sam. Thanks for helpin' my young friend."

Daphne had gone around the buggy to get in on the near side, since the off, or driver's side was nearest the building.

"By the way," she said carelessly as Bessie cramped the rig so that she could put her foot on the step, "Mr. Hondo Horn was here looking for you. Did he find you?"

"What?" Bessie gasped. "Hondo—here? Looking for me? How long since?"

"About an hour I should say."

"Humph! How did you know it was Hondo?"

"Why, I—— Well, the way he asked for you I was sure it was him."

"Get on in. I think you got your wires crossed, dearie. If Rondo had been in town it wouldn't have taken him an hour to look me up."

Daphne blushed, feeling that she had made a fool of herself. But she had been so *sure*.

For half a mile Bessie had her hands full trying to hold the rollicking little mares down to a trot.

" You'll be glad I didn't let you run, you idiots, before you get home," she told them.

Another mile and they overtook half a dozen lumbering wagons, each drawn by a four-horse team, and piled high with sacks of grain.

Bessie turned out in the sagebrush to pass them. Each driver, in turn, waved at them, and Bessie called out, " Keep 'em rolling, boys."

Five miles farther on they met a canvas covered mountain hack coming at a fast speed. Bessie turned out to let the rig past, and the driver waved.

" Stage," Bessie explained. " Can't make the U.S. mail give the road."

It wasn't the kind of stage Daphne had seen in pictures, and she was glad to escape the ride.

" Listen, honey," Bessie said suddenly, " about that five hundred dollars. We're likely to be on the opposite sides of the fence, but we can still be friends—I hope. If I were you I'd put that money in George A. Kump's bank for a while, and not be in too big a hurry to turn it over to ' Slick ' Abel."

Daphne said nothing.

" All right, I'll not stick my neck out again," Bessie shrugged presently.

The team had slowed long since to a lazy trot, except up the hills where Bessie let them walk, but it was only a little after noon when they crossed a low pass near the snub end of a ridge, and saw a small town of perhaps fifteen hundred people nestling in a cove three-quarters of a mile distant. The road wound round the side of a gulch, and beyond the town a small river glistened like silver. The wind had ceased to blow a long time back, and the ride had not been at all uncomfortable. Daphne roused herself, suddenly realizing that she had been half asleep.

" There 'tis," Bessie said. " That's Highline, county seat of Aspen County. Esmeralda took it pretty hard when they moved the courthouse up here. That yellow stone building out there toward the river is the courthouse. They keep the prisoners on the upstairs floor."

That was what Daphne wanted to know. That was where Willard would be.

As they entered the town there was a big barn off the right with a sign,

LIVERY STABLE

painted on the square false front in big white letters.

Adjoining it was a smaller building with a similar false front bearing the sign,

BELL FEED & LIVERY CO.

" That's me," Bessie said. " Livery, feed, and trouble. I've had to manage it ever since my husband was killed last fall."

" Oh, I'm sorry," Daphne said. " I haven't been very gracious. I want to pay you for the ride."

" Nix, I'm not competing with the stage company. We'll just drive up to the hotel and let you out. I live in that little white house across the street. Come and see me any time you feel like it."

Bessie turned a corner to stop in front of a hotel much newer and smarter looking than the Commercial in Esmeralda. Strangely enough it was named, THE ESMERALDA HOTEL.

" Oh, oh ! " Bessie exclaimed. " Looks like trouble."

The same big man whom Daphne had mistaken for Hondo Horn back in Esmeralda stepped off the porch in front of the hotel and came to meet them. He raised a finger. His horse, still white with lather, was tied to a hitching-post a few rods away.

" Well, Bessie, I beat you in," he said.

" Seems like it," Bessie said, without stopping.

" I bought your oats," the man said. " Want to pay you for 'em."

" What ? " Bessie stopped her team abruptly. " You want to what ? "

" Pay for them six wagon-loads of oats," the man said, drawing out a cheque-book. " Seven hundred and twenty-eight bushels at eighty cents a bushel comes to $582.40. Same price you sell 'em for here, but I paid your drivers myself."

Bessie Bell transferred the reins to her left hand and reached for the buggy-whip in its socket with her right.

" Them oats are going to be unloaded in my warehouse,

and not one bushel of them are you going to get, Rumel Thornberry. I told you before I'd sell no feed to the likes of you."

"Guess again, Bessie," the man grinned. "My money is as good as anybody else's. I just took the liberty of riding around your wagons and tellin' the drivers you and me had made a deal. The wagons are on their way to my ranch now."

"Then you git 'em back here, Thornberry, and do it fast," Bessie said furiously, her bosom heaving with anger.

"Not me," Thornberry refused laconically. "An' them wagons will be unloaded before you can overtake 'em. An' if you try to move the oats away I'll have you arrested for trespass."

"Why, you low-down thievin' skunk!" Bessie cried, and raised the buggy whip. "Swish!" It was directed at the man's face, but he leaped in so that the middle of it struck him across the shoulder. He was on the side nearest Daphne.

Thornberry caught the whip with one hand and tore it out of Bessie's hand, almost toppling her out of the rig, as she rose to her feet.

"Nobody, man or woman, can take a whip to me," Thornberry ground out and hurled the whip into the street. The team leaped ahead, but he caught the reins ahead of Bessie's hand, and leaping back just in time to avoid the wheel, gave a vicious jerk which brought the tender-bitted driving mares back on their haunches.

Maddened by the pain the animals tried to rear. Thornberry jerked savagely again, on one rein this time. The buggy cramped, and the next moment tipped over on its side in the street.

Daphne screamed as she felt herself falling, then found her mouth full of the dirt of the street. She was not hurt, for she had fallen on top of Bessie, and the rig didn't come on over. Thornberry, however, threw away the reins, or dropped them, and the frightened animals started to run. The light buggy, even on its side, failed to impede them at all. The bystanders scrambled to get out of the way while women and children screamed. The buggy turned back on its wheels for an instant, but as the runaways turned a corner it whirled completely over, smashing the top, and the wild running mares disappeared, dragging the buggy behind them with all four wheels in the air.

Daphne scrambled to her feet, spitting out dirt, while agonizingly aware that her face was completely covered with the stuff, and that she was a sight. Her fears that Bessie had been badly hurt were disipated when that lady got up almost as quickly as Daphne did.

There were quite a number of people on the street, but none of them seemed disposed to intervene until a man rushed from the door of a rock building a few rods down the street and strode toward them.

Daphne was not even aware of him until she heard his voice. "I saw that, Thornberry," he said. "How do you want it, you skunk—hot lead, or fists?"

"Hondo! Keep out of this," Bessie screamed, but the man seemed to sweep both women out of his way without even touching them.

Daphne got a frightened glimpse of a grim, bronzed face, a pair of implacable grey eyes, and a great, angry vein swelling up the middle of the man's forehead, and then she saw only a graceful not too flat back covered tightly by a grey shirt.

Daphne wanted to scream, but she couldn't have uttered a sound, even had her mouth not been full of mud.

Chapter III — Street Fight

Humel Thornberry stood flat-footed, with clenched fists by his side. He wore a sixgun, but he wasn't touching it. The black, bone handle of a gun projected from the holster at the thigh of the other man, but he wasn't touching it either, nor were his fists clenched.

"Hold on, Horn," Thornberry warned. "This don't concern you."

"You think you can go around upsetting ladies in the street and get away with it? Not while I'm here, Thornberry," Horn said. His voice was deep and incisive, but it didn't rumble.

"Keep away, Horn—I'm warning you," Thornberry almost desperately piped up in his shrill voice. "When I'm roused I'm a *killer*."

Somebody grabbed Daphne then and jerked her toward the sidewalk. When she could turn her head again the two men were so intertwined as to seem one body. But not for long. A splat that made her wince, unaccustomed as she was to the sound of hard fist meeting soft flesh, sounded, and she saw Thornberry apparently running backward on his heels for eight or ten feet before he sat down heavily in the street. His hand went to his mouth then, and came away red with his own blood.

"Touch that gun, Thornberry, and I'll nail you to the street with a bullet," Hondo Horn grated. "Unbuckle it where you are and throw it away."

Thornberry's hands came slowly around to his middle and he unbuckled his gun belt and tossed both gun and belt three feet away from him. He got slowly to his feet then while Hondo Horn unbuckled his gun belt and let it fall at his feet.

Daphne found herself pinned against the wall of the hotel by a massive back, and a huge hand upon her arm. She had to crane her neck around to see past that enormous body. Looking up she could see a wrinkled red neck surmounted by a thatch of iron-grey hair. She was still spitting to rid her mouth of the taste of street debris.

Only when both combatants were relieved of their weapons did Daphne's captor step from in front of her, and then he retained his grasp on her arm. She sensed, vaguely, that whoever he was, he had been shielding her from a possible wild bullet from Thornberry's gun with his own body.

Hondo Horn was standing still, while Thornberry advanced upon him with a slow, crablike motion, pawing out awkwardly with his left hand while he kept the right cocked for a devastating full length swing.

When their hands were close enough to touch Thornberry began to circle, still with that crablike mode of locomotion. Daphne saw now that Thornberry was the heavier and taller of the two antagonists. Horn only looked big because of a deceptive width of shoulder. By now she realized that this was the Hondo Horn who was trying to lay his own crime on to her brother's shoulders. She should have been hating him, hoping for the other man to win; but she wasn't. When they suddenly exploded into action again, with each man grunting from the impact of the other's hard but unskilled blows she found herself a partisan in the Horn camp.

The crowd was divided. Some were yelling, "Hit him, Hondo!" Others frenziedly imploring, "Kill him, Rumel! Smash him!"

One of those cocked right fists of Thornberry's suddenly landed and Horn appeared to soar through the air to come down upon his side, his head missing the edge of the wooden sidewalk by no more than six inches. Had it struck there the fight would have been over.

The huge old man holding Daphne's arm groaned aloud, and Daphne glanced up quickly. She thought she had never seen such a homely face. It was broad and flat except for a tremendous nose and thick lips stained by tobacco juice. In his excitement the old man's jaws were working frenziedly. But he wasn't saying anything.

Horn sprang to his feet—he had to or have his ribs caved in by his foe's boots. He caught a cuff to the right of the head and another to the left. His eyes were glassy. As though sensing the sudden finish of the fight the partisans stilled.

Somehow Horn circled his foe and got away from the sidewalk toward which Thornberry was trying to force him. He stopped, and again the cocked right came whistling through the air. Horn ducked, and the blow went over his head. His toes gripped the ground then, and he dug one fist and then the other into his enemy's mid-riff.

Thornberry grunted explosively at each blow, and doubled over with folded arms to protect his stomach. Then a savage left upper-cut collided with his jaw so hard that he must have thought his head was being torn off. He turned half over as he fell, and landed on his face. He lay there, kicking convulsively as he tried to get wind back into his lungs.

Hondo Horn stood back, shaking his head and spitting out blood.

Finally Thornberry turned over and sat with his arms clasping his stomach. He, too, was bleeding from mouth and nose. He gasped a couple of times then got out weakly, "Wait I've had enough. I'm whipped."

"Why, he's as yaller as a bitch pup," one of his late henchmen said disgustedly.

"You may be whipped, but I'm not through yet," Hondo Horn panted. "You've still got a bill to pay, and some apologies to make."

"That's all right, Hondo ; I'll take over from here," Bessie Bell said suddenly. "Thanks just the same though."

"Get his gun, Hondo, and see that he don't get another one before he leaves town," said Daphne's protector, and Hondo nodded.

The ugly old man looked down at Daphne and grinned, displaying yellow, uneven teeth. "You better go wash your face, sis," he advised. "Right now you're homelier than I am."

"Just a minute, George A.," Bessie spoke up. "I want you to meet my young friend. This is Daphne Dixon, Willard Dixon's sister. She rode out from town with me. Miss Dixon, this is George A. Kump, our big bank and cattle tycoon."

"Well, you're not exactly a stranger then, Miss Dixon," Kump said. "But I still think you ought to wash your face."

"Come this way, dearie," Bessie said. "We both need to wash up."

She led the way through the lobby to the desk.

"Give us a room, Nick," she told the Greek behind the desk. "A good one. Miss Dixon will be staying in it."

"I take you up myself," Nick offered.

They climbed a stair and Nick threw open the door of a front room. "Bath'n everything," he said. "And a fine view."

"Just never mind charging for the view," Bessie said. "Get out and leave us clean up."

Daphne went straight to a mirror and gave a dismayed cry at sight of her face. She had unconsciously licked the dirt from around her mouth as far as her tongue could reach, but the rest was a dingy brown mass of dirt, and her hair had given way from its moorings. A comb, held by one tooth, dangled drunkenly over one ear.

"Well, you sure got a reception in Highline, honey," Bessie said. "Met most of the talked about people, too. George A. Kump, Hondo Thorn, Rumel Thornberry—and me. Had Slick Abel, Brig Dow, and Ez Thornberry showed up you'd have met 'em all."

Daphne, however, was thinking about only one man. Hondo Horn. Her brother's enemy, and the man whom Bessie Bell was confessedly in love with. Even as she scrubbed the dirt from her face she kept thinking about him. Since Thornberry had been so brutish it was natural that she should have wanted Horn to win the fight, of course. But need she have wanted him to win so *hard*? Her anxiety had been, not to see Thornberry punished as it was dread lest Hondo Horn be hurt. There was something wrong somewhere, she knew.

She got her face clean, and her hair fixed someway. But she needed fresh clothing.

"My valises!" she gasped suddenly. "What—what am I going to do?"

Bessie brought her half submerged face out of the wash bowl. "Hunh? What did you say? Guess I got water in my ears."

"I've got no clothes. Everything I've got was in that runaway."

"That Rumel Thornberry! If I'd remembered your grips I'd have went over and kicked him while he was down. My dresses may be a little kind of loose, but you'll look decent in one of 'em anyway."

Daphne bit her lip. She didn't want to become indebted any more to Bessie Bell, but she could see no way out of it.

"This trouble with Mr Thornberry—he didn't have any right to send your wagons where you didn't want them to go, did he?"

"The Thornberrys sort of make up their own rules as they go along, and so do I. That's why we don't hitch. Been a man in my place, my late husband, Tim Bell, say, and he would have sold the Thornberrys all the grain they wanted to buy so long as they paid the price. But me, bein' a woman, when I don't like somebody I just don't do business with them. I can get grain for four-bits a hundred cheaper than Thornberry can get it—if he can buy it at all. This country is too high and frosty to raise grain, and I've got the only feed store business in here. So I guess it made Rumel kind of mad when I told him I wouldn't sell him anything at any price."

"But why?" Daphne persisted.

"Honey, I hate to tell you. You see, I like you. I think you're a good kid. But I like Hondo Horn a lot better, and his enemies are my enemies. The Thornberrys are trying to clear your brother, and hang that stealing on to Hondo."

"Oh," Daphne murmured almost inaudibly.

"There you have it, Miss Dixon. We're in opposite camps like I said. And it goes back a lot further than you know. I've got an awful bad fault. I'm truthful. I wear my darned heart on my sleeve. When Hondo Horn came in here a few years ago and started working for George A. Kump I was a green girl going with a nice lad named Tim Bell. I went overboard for Hondo, and I've been that way ever since."

"Yet you married Tim Bell?"

"I married him. But not until after I'd throwed my rope at Hondo, and missed. I told Tim exactly how I felt, and I promised to try to be a good wife to him if he wanted me. I had a little money I'd inherited, enough to start this feed and livery business, and Tim liked it.

"We got married, and I done my best to forget Hondo, but he was always around darn him, and him and Tim remained close friends. Then Tim got killed one day, out hunting deer. A stray shot hit him. We never did find out who fired it. Hondo was awful kind. He'd got to be George A.'s foreman in the meantime, but he helped me carry on my business. I used to hope he'd fall for me, and sometimes I think maybe he does love me a little, but he never speaks of it. Anyway, the Bell woman can take it. But when I saw Thornberrys doin' him dirt I fought for him in every way I could."

"I'm sorry," Daphne said lamely, because she couldn't think of anything else to say.

"The root of it is this. The Thornberrys live back in the hills with a lot of other riff-raff who run little cow outfits. They've clashed with the K Bar K ever since they came in here. George A. is getting old, and they think if it wasn't for Hondo they could wreck the K Bar K and steal its range. Your brother Willard ain't the first honest cowboy they've corrupted, but he is the first one to actually put Hondo in danger. Now I guess you know where we both stand."

Bessie's face was clean, but her shoulders drooped with discouragement or weariness.

"Yes, I guess we do," Daphne said. "Thanks for telling me, and I won't abuse your confidence."

"Oh, hell, it's no secret—the way I feel about Hondo," Bessie said. "Everybody can see it, except him."

For a while after Bessie had gone Daphne busied herself brushing the dirt from her dress and hat. Nothing had been seriously damaged, and she would be presentable, but this wasn't the outfit she wanted to wear when she saw Willard.

Her window overlooked the yellow stone courthouse. For all she knew Willard might be standing at one of the windows she could see right now. She hastily gulped back an involuntary sob that came tearing up her throat. She couldn't give way to feminine tears and hysterics. This was a hard country, and if she was going to do her brother any good she would have to be hard, too.

Willard wouldn't want to see her. She knew that the lawyer had written without his consent. He had probably hoped that she would never find out about his disgrace. He was capable of a cold cruel aloofness that was as hard to cut as glass.

What bothered her now was a creeping doubt of his innocence. He had never been a thief, and she couldn't believe he was cowardly enough to put the blame for his actions on someone else. After all, she told herself firmly, Willard was her brother; these other people were strangers.

She got dressed again finally and started resolutely for the door. She would have to find Attorney Abel first, and then arrange a meeting with Willard.

As she reached for the door-knob somebody knocked. Startled, she drew back, and was angry at herself for being so jittery. It was probably Bessie sending over some clothes.

"Come in," she called.

The door opened and she saw a pair of legs and her two battered valises. Her eyes rolled upward and rested upon the face of Hondo Horn. He came on in without apology.

CHAPTER IV — KNEE-TAPPING LAWYER

"OH," Daphne said weakly, "you brought my bags." She glanced at his face, then swiftly away. It wasn't a stern, angry face as she had seen it before, and the great rope of a vein through the middle of his forehead had disappeared. His grey eyes smiled, and she noticed a slight humorous droop in the corner of one of them. The other, however, was badly swollen. His lips were puffed out and cut and there were other abrasions on his face as a result of the recent fight.

"This one," he said, turning one heavy valise around, "got pretty badly ripped. I hope you didn't lose anything."

"I'm lucky to get them back at all," she said. "Set them over there, will you?"

She felt foolish standing in the middle of the room so she sat down on the edge of the bed. Hondo carefully placed the valises on the floor and removed his wide-brimmed grey Stetson. She noticed that his hair was wavy, and it was just a shade lighter than black. He showed no inclination to rush away.

"The—horses—were they hurt?" she asked.

"Hardly a scratch. They shucked what was left of the buggy about a mile out, and circled back to the livery stable with two collars and one tug." He was looking steadily into her face, but with an expression in his eyes that kept the look from being a stare.

"You know," he said after a pause, "you sure looked funny out there in the street—like you was made up for a minstrel act."

He chuckled softly, and Daphne's face reddened. She didn't know how he had possibly found time to see how she looked. She didn't think he had taken his eyes off Rumel Thornberry.

"I don't suppose you know who I am?" she said stiffly.

"Oh, yes. Bessie told me you were Willard Dixon's sister. I'm sorry Willard got into trouble."

She wished he would get his eyes off her face. She was tempted to seize a water glass and hurl it across the room just to see if she couldn't make him look away.

"I wish you had felt that way before you got him into trouble," she shot out.

"It wouldn't be much of a sister who wouldn't stick up for her own brother," he stated without offence. "If I can do anything for you, Miss Dixon, let me know."

He got out of the room easily, a little trick which she had noticed most cowboys had trouble doing. She had the angry feeling that she had looked worse here in the room than down on the street with her face covered with dirt.

She began unpacking her valises. Some of the things in the torn valise were soiled, but otherwise things were undamaged. She changed into a black skirt and a white shirt-waist, re-arranged her hair, and finally went down stairs.

"I'd like to arrange to keep that room," she told Nick Cropopolos.

"That's all right, Miss Dixon," Nick said. "I stick you up eight dollars a week with bath. Meals five dollars a week unless you like good grub—then you go across the street."

Nick was proud of his cuisine, and liked to call attention to it by running the place down.

"I'm sure it will be fine," she said. "Could you tell me where I can find Attorney Aaron Abel?"

"Office over the drug store. If you don't find him there look in the Senate Saloon."

Daphne located the one drug store in Highline and climbed a stairway leading from the street. The upstairs appeared to be the principal office building in the town, and she had a little trouble locating a rear room with Aaron Abel's name on the door. She could hear voices inside, but she knocked timidly.

"Come in," a voice called.

As she opened the door she saw a middle-sized man with a bald head and a thin, narrow face closing an inner door. Despite his bald head he didn't look old.

"Mr. Abel?" she asked.

"Yes, yes, of course. And you are Miss Daphne Dixon, my client's sister. I've already heard you were in town."

"I guess I made quite a sensational entrance—on my nose," she said a bit grimly, as she accepted the lawyer's moist handclasp.

"It wouldn't have happened if we had known it was you," Abel smirked.

"Did you say 'we'?" Daphne queried.

"Well, just a figure of speech, my dear. A lawyer always identifies himself with his client. Mr. Thornberry, who certainly had sufficient provocation for what he did, is also my client. I might add that he and his brother Ezra are battling very hard to clear your brother of the false charges against him."

The lawyer had a soft and seductive voice. After all he was Willard's attorney. And if the Thornberrys were really Willard's friends she could perhaps overlook the fall she had taken. According to Bessie Bell's own story her refusal to sell grain to the man had been utterly highhanded.

"I appreciate you letting me know about Willard," she said. "How soon can it be arranged for me to see him?"

"Very soon, I'm sure, but first I think you and Rumel Thornberry ought to get things fixed up between you. Will you come out, Rumel?"

Involuntarily Daphne recoiled a step when Thornberry came out of the inner office. With his face badly beaten he was even more repulsive than before. Contrasted with Hondo Horn the man got much the worst of it. But Daphne tried to overcome her repugnance with the thought that he was Willard's friend. Abel performed the introduction gracefully.

"Glad to metcha, miss," Thornberry grunted. "'F I'd knowed who you was in that buggy I'd waited till yuh got out 'fore tacklin' Bess Bell."

"You see, Miss Dixon, the last thing we expected was to see you hob-nobbing with your brother's enemies," Abel put in reproachfully.

"Well, Mrs. Bell had offered me the ride before she knew who I was, and it's hard to think she is an enemy."

"She's a——" Thornberry began.

"Don't say it, Rumel," Abel interposed quickly. "Bessie is all right. She's just being used as a tool by old man Kump and Hondo Horn."

"She's costin' me plenty just the same—or would if I hadn't got that grain," Thornberry growled.

"You mean you can force her to sell you that grain against her will?" Daphne queried.

"I'd like to see her try to git it back," the man grinned; the bumps and abrasions on his face making the grin a horrible grimace.

"Well, you just remember what I told you, Rumel, and sit tight." Abel dismissed the rancher hurriedly.

When Thornberry had gone Abel ushered Daphne into his private office. It was a dingy, unkempt looking den, with a desk battered by the attorney's heels, and several shelves of lawbooks covered with dust a quarter of an inch thick.

"Have a seat, my dear," Abel bowed. When she was seated he dragged his big swivel chair around to the end of the desk where he was closer than Daphne liked.

"What I want to know," she said pointedly, "is what chance Willard has of acquittal?"

"I'm glad you brought that up, Miss Dixon, or may I call you Daphne?"

She disliked too much familiarity, but felt compelled to say, "Certainly."

"In the first place, my dear"—that was even worse than Daphne, she thought—"your brother is only a wild kid who happens to be a mere pawn in a big chess game, in fact control of this entire country. The question is whether it shall remain George A. Kump's feudal domain, or a country with equal rights for all."

Daphne pushed her chair back a little as the lawyer's moist hand descended for the second time upon her slender knee. Despite his seductive voice he wasn't quite the type she would have pictured as a great champion of democracy.

"By the aid of this *hired gunman,* Hondo Horn, and his crew of ruffians, Kump has managed to terrorize the smaller ranchers such as the Thornberrys, keeping them from expansion, and in many cases actually robbing them of their property," Abel charged.

"You mean to say that this Mr. Kump had a hand in framing my brother?" Daphne queried. It would have been more believable if she had not already met Kump, the big, red-necked man who had placed himself in front of her when there was danger of bullets beginning to fly.

" Frankly, we don't know. It's just possible that Horn was feathering his own nest at his employer's expense. It's also possible that he was privy to the whole transaction for the purpose of getting your brother in his power. At any rate that doesn't concern us. The point is we want proof that Hondo Horn employed your brother to feed those cattle. If we can get it Willard will be acquitted. If they can prove that he bought that hay himself and fed it to K Bar K cattle then they'll send him over the road for five years at least."

Daphne could not repress a shudder at thought of what this would mean to Willard. She began to understand that the lawyer was right about Willard being only a pawn in a big game. The seductive voice was having its effect. Hatred against Hondo Horn began to crystallize within her like slush rapidly changing to ice.

" The point is, Daphne, that your brother's fate depends entirely upon the question of whose money paid for the hay. If "—the lawyer hitched his chair a trifle closer, and emphasized each word with a tap of his finger upon Daphne's knee—" we could produce a witness who would swear that he saw Hondo Horn give Willard five hundred dollars, telling him at the same time to buy Sep Kohler's hay, we would have the case in the bag, and we could send Horn over the road."

" But—but is there such a witness ? " Daphne blurted.

" There is," Abel said impressively. " The trouble is he is a saloon bum, easily frightened, and he is afraid Hondo Horn would kill him if he told the truth."

" But couldn't he be forced——"

" We could put him on the stand, and if he denied everything it would fix our case. No, force wouldn't work with Bill Burgess, but money would. I've talked to him. For a thousand dollars in cash the fellow will go on the stand. Of course, there are some other little details. We've got to promise him protection until he can get out of the country. The trouble is we haven't got the thousand dollars—or have we ? "

Abel's small, rather beady blue eyes were now fixed compellingly upon hers.

" I—I—only have five hundred dollars," Daphne disclosed. " If it will do any good——"

"It's not enough. If you really want to save your brother you must raise another five hundred."

"I don't know where I could get it," Daphne faltered.

"I'm serving practically without fee," Slick Abel said. "Your brother was broke. All I get is what Ez and Rumel Thornberry have donated simply because they like Willard and hate Hondo Horn. But that isn't much—a mere fifty dollars up to now."

Daphne's soul revolted against being beholden to a man like Rumel Thornberry. But she could swallow her pride to save Willard that five years in the penitentiary.

"I'll try to raise the money, Mr. Abel," she said, rising. "I don't know how, but I'll raise it someway. And enough to pay back the Thornberrys."

"That's the spirit I like," Abel smiled, seizing one of her hands in both of his and crushing it softly and moistly. "Now you go back to your hotel and let me prepare Willard for an interview. I think it would be wise to let him sleep over it and see him to-morrow."

"I'm awfully anxious to see him."

"I know But he didn't want you to find out, and he is sure to fly off the handle. He must have time to cool off," the lawyer insisted.

"Well, good day then," Daphne said, releasing her hand.

"Good day, my dear. And don't be discouraged. I think it will be entirely possible to find a way for you to raise that other five hundred dollars. Yes, indeed I do—entirely possible."

He followed to the head of the stairs, and watched her trim figure down to the street level.

"Entirely possible," he repeated softly to himself as he returned to his office.

CHAPTER V "I MIGHT HAVE BEEN A BUM"

HONDO HORN stopped in at the livery stable after he had delivered Daphne's valises at the hotel. Bessie, in a checkered red and white print dress, was in her office in the front of the feed store.

"Hello, messenger boy," she said, looking up with a smile.

"Not messenger boy—Bell boy," he grinned.

"If it were only true," she sighed. "What do you think of my little friend now she's cleaned up?"

"Quite a filly," Hondo returned casually. "Too bad she's got such a louse of a brother."

"It is. Hondo, I'm scared."

"You should be—deliberately starting a row with Rumel Thornberry and costing yourself money."

"It's not that, and you know it. As long as I run this business I'll run it. I'm afraid for you."

"You mean about the fight to-day, or the Dixon case?"

"Both. The Thornberrys are back of both, and with Slick Abel to supply brains they're dangerous. If a jury believes that kid they'll have you arrested. If they don't believe him the Thornberrys will get you some other way."

"I don't take either one seriously," Hondo said easily. "Look, Bess: What twelve men in their right minds would believe I'd steal fifty or sixty cows from my own boss? George A. certainly don't. As for Ez and Rumel they'll step over the line some day, and when they do I'll be ready for 'em."

"Have you thought what effect that girl will have on a jury when she tells 'em what a little angel her precious brother has always been? She's the kind of a gal men fall for, Hondo. Lookit to-day. When it looked like shots might be going to fly did anybody worry about Bessie? Not that you could notice. But who put himself in front of little Daphne to protect her with his own carcass? Nobody else but George A. Kump himself."

Hondo laughed. "Everybody knows your hide is tough enough to turn bullets," he said. "I do feel sorry for the kid. I suppose Willard's only trouble is that he's weak. I know he didn't have a dollar, so somebody else gave him the money to buy that hay, and somebody else drove those cattle there. I suppose I know, too, who it was."

"And they wouldn't have risked such a thing if they hadn't been pretty sure they could make it stick, Hondo. What does the prosecuting attorney think?"

"Thatcher thinks he can get a conviction. But I wish that sister of Dixon's hadn't showed up."

"Brother, so do I," Bessie said earnestly.

Hondo seated himself on the corner of his desk. "You know, Bessie," he said, "you raised hell with me—you and Tim. Always preachin' that I ought to settle down and be respectable. If it hadn't been for you two I wouldn't be in this mess now. I'd be a happy and independent bum."

"I wonder. You're always bragging about what a tramp you were until I ruined your life by persuading you to hold down an honest job. But it occurs to me now that I don't know a thing about what you were before you came here, you close-mouthed coyote. Why, I don't even know your first name. I know your parents never christened you Hondo."

"They thought of hanging me at birth, but my head kept slipping through the noose so they called me Hondo."

"Sometimes I wonder if you wasn't a bad egg before you landed here," she said. She noted a quick darkening of his face, and added instantly, "Anyway, it's all right with me."

He laughed. "Thanks, Bess. I reckon you're about the best friend I ever had. It's small return to let you think you weaned me away from a life of crime."

"By the way, I saw that new puncher of yours the other day," Bessie said.

"You mean Pat Young?"

"Don't know his name. He looks plenty hard."

"I've got an idea that's the kind of men we're going to need. Look, Bessie: Things have got to come to a showdown around here. That outfit is goin' to keep on horse-flyin' the K Bar K until we've got to turn tail and run, or turn around and kick hell out of 'em. It can't be any other way. The old man savvies that. He don't really care whether he bosses the country or not, but he knows if he don't Slick Abel, Brig Dow, and the Thornberrys will. So he's got to fight."

Both were suddenly earnest. Bessie doodled with her pencil while he talked. When he finished she looked up.

"I know. And it scares hell out of me. Neither Ez nor Rumel are smart enough to know their own power, but Slick

Abel and Brig Dow are. If we lose this trial, if young Dixon is freed, then there'll be a big howl, 'Down with the K Bar K.'"

"It's a fact," Hondo admitted. "Sheriff Watson is a good man, but George A. put him in office. They'll run Brig Dow against him next fall, and that'll mean war in the hills, unless we just set back and let 'em steal our cattle. If I know the old man we'll never do that."

"And that's why you hired this Pat Young?" she asked.

"Not exactly."

"He's a gunman, ain't he?"

"Maybe—in a way. But I've still not got to the point where I have to hire somebody else to do my fighting for me. Which ain't to say I wouldn't mind havin' Pat side me if I had to face Ez and Rumel at the same time."

"Anyway, no matter how sorry we may feel for this Dixon girl, Hondo, we've got to send her brother to the pen. Refusing to press the case now would be the same as for you to plead guilty of trying to frame him."

"Who said anything about dropping the case?" he demanded.

"Excuse me. Maybe my mind reading ain't so good to-day," Bessie said with a shade of bitterness. "You going out to the ranch now?"

"Thought I would."

"Oh, I must tell you something that happened this morning in Esmeralda. Rumel Thornberry was down there and little bright-eyes thought he was you. She actually told me that Hondo Horn wanted to see me."

"So that's the kind of hombre she thinks I am," Hondo mused. "I must see about changing her ideas."

"Will you get the hell out of here and let me work?" Bessie said, half angrily. "I'm fixing up a bill of damages for Sheriff Watson to present to Rumel Thornberry when he goes out to replevin those oats."

"Sure you shouldn't just let the grain business drop—providing he pays you?"

"Not on your life! This is my private feud. I said I wouldn't sell the Thornberrys any grain for their dirty hogs, and I won't."

Hondo shrugged. "Bet you a pair of silk socks against the price of a beer you don't get your oats back," he offered.

"You're on," Bessie said.

Hondo stood in the doorway a moment, as though he might

have something more to say, then mounted his horse and rode over to the Highline State Bank. It was long since closed, but a rap on the window caused a shade inside to be raised, and a moment later the door opened. George A. Kump was alone in the bank.

"Dammit, I'm a cowman, not a dad-blamed bookkeeper," Kump fumed. "Way that cashier of mine keeps books half the time I don't know whether I owe money or whether somebody owes me."

"Why don't you hire more help?"

"I would in a minute if I could get somebody."

"I remember Willard Dixon tellin' me last summer that his sister worked in a bank."

Kump swung round abruptly. "Hunh?" he blurted. "You suggestin' that I hire the sister of the lyin' scoundrel who stole my cows and tried to blame it on you to keep books in my bank?"

"Why not? The best chance we've got is to make Dixon weaken and tell who put him up to what he done. If we could get on the good side of his sister she might win him over," Hondo argued.

Kump stared. "Nope, she'd never take a job here."

"It wouldn't do any hurt to try."

"Humph! What you make of Rumel Thornberry quittin' like he did to-day. He could have made a better fight than he did." Kump switched the topic of conversation.

"I don't know. I just figgered he hurt easy," Hondo answered.

"I ain't sayin' he could lick you, but he could have took more," Kump said. "You whipped him. If he should provoke you some time, or Ez either, it might go a long way in establishin' self defence if one of 'em happened to plug you."

"Between you and Bessie, I've sure got a pair to do my thinkin' for me," Hondo said, obviously a little irked.

"We just got to be careful," Kump said patiently. "We've got to keep this country decent. The Thornberrys wouldn't last long if they ever took over, but they would sure raise Ned for a while. We've got to watch our step."

"Any orders before I leave?" Hondo asked.

"None. Just don't let anybody provoke you until this trial is over."

Hondo rode out to the main K Bar K ranch ten miles distant. It was a big spread and employed more than twenty men. It was after dark when he arrived, and the men had had supper. He went into the bunkhouse where most of the men not at line camps were playing cards.

"Where's Pat Young?" he asked when he missed the newest acquisition to the crew.

"Dunno, Hondo," Spike Williams answered. "He ain't got in yet."

"Maybe he got lost," Owen Denny, the youngest member of the crew, volunteered. "Say, Hondo, what happened to yore face?"

Everybody in the bunkhouse squared round to survey the ravages of battle.

"Just had an argument with Rumel Thornberry," Hondo said shortly. "I'm goin' to bed. I want the whole gang of you up at five o'clock in the morning. We're takin' the last bunch of feeders into Swan Basin."

Silence followed his departure for all of a minute, then Owen Denny burst out, "Say, what do yuh think? Did Rumel Thornberry lick him?"

"Musta done, or he'd said more about it," suggested Nate Barstow.

"Like hell!" Spike Williams scoffed. "If Hondo had taken a lickin' he'd be wearin' a lot more marks than he's carryin' now. Rumel couldn't lick one side of him."

"That fight's been comin' on fer two years, an' we hadda miss it," Owen mourned. "I do love a good fight."

"Looks to me like you might find yoreself in one," Ben Rambeau, the oldest man on the crew, remarked. Ben was fifty-five, with an enormous red moustache, and a dome that was bald as a billard ball. He did pretty much as he pleased on the K Bar K.

"Who with?" Owen challenged, picking up a poker with mock belligerence.

"I ain't bein' funny," Ben said. "Didn't you hear what he said? We're takin' a bunch of cattle up Swan Crick to-morrow. In case you've forgotten that's above where the Thornberrys live. And they've served notice on us to keep all K Bar K stuff outa there."

Chapter VI A Job with the Enemy

Slick Abel stopped in at the Esmeralda Hotel about ten o'clock the next morning and told Nick Cropopolos that he wanted to see Miss Dixon.

" She been down here twenty times a'ready," Nick said. " You wait five minutes and you can't miss."

" Jittery, eh ? " Slick smiled.

" W'y not ? Got a brother goin' to the pen, ain't it ? "

" What ? Whoever told you that, Nick ? Willard Dixon is coming clear as sure as we're standing here."

" Don't kill me laughing. What somebody is goin' believe Hondo Horn would pull a trick like that ? This Dixon kid, he no good anyway——"

Nick stopped with open mouth as he saw Daphne at the head of the stairs.

She had heard most of Nick's last remark, and it didn't make her feel any better. She had been anxious for the lawyer to come. Meeting Willard was going to be an ordeal, and she wanted it over with.

Abel met her at the bottom step. " Ah, my dear, you look lovely," he said in his most seductive voice. " I hope you rested well."

" Can I see Willard now, Mr. Abel ? " she asked.

" Yes. Visiting hours are in the afternoon, and I almost had to use threats to get the sheriff to relent in this case. He owes his election to George A. Kump, so we don't get any favours from him," he said bitterly.

" How——did Willard take it——my being here ? "

" Frankly, my dear, he called me some pretty unsavoury names till he quieted down. I finally made him see that you would have found out anyway."

Daphne had been out on the street. The spring was still young, and the weather uncertain. The air was full of chill, and she wore a short red jacket, and a white woollen cap over her head.

Slick Abel, wearing a fur-collared overcoat over his formal Prince Albert coat, and with his hat pulled down over his eyes, swung along at her side. Daphne was amazed to find that he wasn't much taller than she was.

It was only a short walk to the yellow courthouse. Just as they entered they met a tall, serious looking young man wearing eye-glasses, coming out.

" Oh, hello, Harold," Abel said genially. " I'd like you to meet a friend of mine, Miss Dixon. Miss Dixon, Mr Thatcher."

Thatcher betrayed surprise, and his acknowledgment of the introduction was anything but cordial. Then he peered at Daphne as if he hadn't seen her clearly before. He was, indeed, near-sighted.

" Harold here, is the unfortunate young lawyer whose duty it is to prosecute your innocent brother," Abel said smilingly.

" I'm sorry, Miss Dixon," Thatcher said nervously. " I hope I'll see you again."

" You will, Harold, you will," Abel cackled as the young prosecutor hurried out.

" Nice young fellow, Thatcher," Abel addressed Daphne. " Let me give you a tip. In law we have to fight with everything we've got. Thatcher takes himself seriously. You could help your brother a great deal getting Harold interested in you. A young man in love is likely to overlook a great many points."

Daphne coloured. She wanted to help Willard in every way she could, but she hadn't contemplated using her physical charms on the prosecuting attorney.

" Can't we see Willard now ? " she asked.

" Of course."

Abel led the way to the sheriff's office. Sheriff Watson, a short, round-shouldered, heavy man with bristling white eyebrows glanced at the lawyer, then allowed his gaze to slide off on to Daphne.

" So this is the girl you've been telling me about, eh, Slick ?" he asked.

" This is Miss Daphne Dixon, Sheriff."

The sheriff didn't offer to shake hands or acknowledge the introduction in any way. He heaved himself to his feet. " I'll take you up," he said. " Sent my deputy out to Thornberry's to replevin some oats for Bessie Bell."

The lawyer smiled a bit contemptuously. Sheriff Watson didn't look very formidable as he led the way rather stiffly to a broad stairway.

Just above the head of the stairs a corridor was blocked off by a steel door. A row of cells bristled on either side. Daphne caught sight of Willard as the sheriff was unlocking the main door. His face was pressed against the bars, and he looked pale and nervous.

"Would it be possible for me to see him alone, Mr. Sheriff?" she asked.

"Why, I reckon so," the sheriff said. "Go right ahead. You can wait in my office Slick. I'll be back after a while."

Slick Abel, however, accompanied them down to the cell.

"Hello, sis," Willard called, with a weak effort to appear nonchalant.

Unable to speak because of a sudden wave of emotion Daphne could only grasp his hand through the bars. When the sheriff opened the door she stepped inside and threw her arms around her brother's neck. They clung together for a minute, neither one able to speak.

"Come on, Slick," the sheriff said dryly, and the lock clicked.

"I'd like to kill that damn shyster for writin' you, sis," Willard said fiercely. "You can't help me any. Why did you come?"

"Because I can help you," she said.

"With your hard-earned money, I suppose. That's the only reason he ever wrote you. Well, you'd just as well set down."

Daphne looked around the bleak little cell, and seated herself on the hard, narrow bunk. Willard sat down beside her and took her hand.

"We're all alone in the world, Willard," she said. "We've got to stand by each other."

"I've been a hell of a brother to you, Daphne. I never was no good. You should forget all about me."

"Willard! You don't mean that you are *guilty*?"

It took half a minute for him to frame a reply, and her doubts accumulated with the seconds.

"No, I didn't steal any cattle," he said finally, and Daphne gave a sigh of relief. "But I got myself into this by being a fool about gambling. If I'd had any sense I could have had a good job with the K Bar K. Hondo wanted me to stay."

"But you wouldn't want to work for a man who would deliberately try to frame you to cover up his own crookedness," she protested.

"Hunh? Oh, yes, I see what you mean. Look, Daphne: You've seen me now. I want you to get on the stage in the morning and go home."

"I won't do it," she refused. "I'm going to stay right here till I see this thing through. If you're innocent we're going to fight it through to the finish. If you're guilty then I want you to tell me so. I'm your sister, and I'll love you just as much as ever. But you must plead guilty so as not to put an innocent man under a cloud. Willard, are you guilty?"

"No!" he almost shouted, leaping to his feet. He took a swift turn in his cooped quarters, then stopped, facing her "All I want is for you to go home and leave me alone."

"That's what you're not going to get," she said spiritedly. "Sit down and hold my hand. That's better. Now we're going to plan your defence."

"Let Slick Abel do that."

"Why does everybody call him that?"

"I dunno. Because he's so slick an' oily, I reckon. And such a crook."

"Willard, he says he has found a witness who saw you get that money from Mr. Horn—the money you bought the hay with. But he says the man won't testify unless he gets a thousand dollars. You know about that, of course?"

"Yeah. It's Bill Burgess. But I don't believe that thousand dollar business. Burgess would perjure himself for ten dollars. He'd swear to any kind of a lie for a hundred dollars."

"But the lawyer said——"

"I know. If he got a thousand dollars he would probably give Burgess fifty of it and keep the rest himself," Willard said cynically

"But the man is afraid of Hondo Horn. He knows he would have to leave the country."

"I guess he would at that. Hondo would murder him."

"Then I'm going to raise that thousand dollars I've five hundred, and I'll get the other five hundred some way," she asserted.

"Oh, forget it, will you?" he said peevishly. "I'll be convicted anyway. Why should you waste your money paying Bill Burgess to lie?"

"To lie? But if he saw Horn hand you the money, how could that——"

"Look, sis," he said earnestly, "don't dirty your hands with this. I've got my story to tell, and I'm going to tell it.

But believe me when I tell you I *want* to be convicted. Now will you go home ? "

It was too much for Daphne. She removed her hand from his, and unconsciously raised it to her mouth while she sat staring at him. He met her look without flinching.

"If you really want to be convicted you must be guilty. In that case why don't you plead that way ? " she asked in a small, dispirited voice.

"I told you I wasn't guilty," he flared. "Oh, for God's sake, Daphne, drop it and go home."

"Not until after the trial."

She got little more out of him. What he said, and his contradictory attitude didn't make sense. She was almost glad when the heavy-footed sheriff arrived to let her out. But she was determined to stay in Highline.

There was very little conversation between her and Abel until they were back in his office. She accepted the chair he offered her but herself placed it at the end of his desk. A moment after he was seated she moved her chair around opposite him. He couldn't very well move his own chair then, so there was no more knee tapping.

"Your brother is a most difficult and unco-operative client," Abel said. "I hope you made him see the necessity for helping in his own defence."

"I can't understand him at all," she replied. "I think he would like to plead guilty, yet he insists that he is innocent."

"Nevertheless, we have got to acquit him in spite of himself."

"If I thought for a minute he was guilty I'd do everything I could to get him to plead that way," she declared.

"He is innocent—I give you my word. But it's going to be hard work making a jury think so. We can't overlook any possible bet. I'll lay my cards on the table, Daphne. Unless I can count on the fullest co-operation from you, then I'll withdraw from the case right now."

"What kind of co-operation are you talking about ? " she demanded.

"There is first the thousand dollars That I've got to have."

"To hire a man to commit perjury ? "

"Whether Burgess is telling the truth or not is no concern of mine, just so he gets on that witness stand and says he saw Hondo Horn give your brother five hundred dollars. I'm assuming he is telling the truth."

" Willard says it's a lie."

" Perhaps your brother will be lying, too, when he swears Horn gave him the money. How do you know he isn't? But he will swear to it."

" Mr. Abel, I have only five hundred dollars. I'll turn it over to you for my brother's defence, and if I can get a job I'll give you every cent I can earn. How you spend it, I suppose, is no concern of mine."

" It's got to be a thousand dollars," he said stubbornly. " I can borrow the other five hundred for you on your note. You can pay it back later."

" Who would loan me money ? " she asked sceptically.

" I will. I'll give you six months to pay it back. I've got the note all made out. And the money right here in my desk."

" But why should you give the money to me if I'm going to give it right back to you ? "

" Because I'm an honest man, and I'm not going to have you and your brother claiming that I perhaps gave Burgess a hundred dollars and pocketed the rest," he smiled grimly. " You are going to give Burgess the money yourself. And get a receipt from him."

Daphne felt as if she were teetering on the edge of a pit filled with sharpened sticks, but she didn't know which way to move. If she acceded she felt that she would be putting herself into some sort of trap; she didn't know what. But if she refused Willard would be convicted. She was in a position where she would have to go all the way, or leave Willard to his fate.

" What else am I supposed to do ? " she asked to gain time.

" For one thing you can play up to Harold Thatcher. Also, if you can, maintain friendly relations with Bessie Bell. Bessie knows everything that goes on in the enemy camp, and she may drop something."

" Why not just carry on a flirtation with Hondo Horn himself ? " she asked sardonically.

Abel took her seriously. " You think you could ? That would be great. We'd be sure to win the case."

" But what if he wouldn't tell me anything ? "

" You leave that to me."

" I'd like to think things over," she pleaded. " I'm a little dizzy."

" There's nothing to think over," he denied. " Either you

want to help your brother, or you don't. If you do, sign this note."

Daphne drew a long breath and accepted the pen he was holding out. She wrote her name, and Abel carefully put the note into his wallet. Then he counted out five hundred dollars in bills.

"Here's what I want you to do," he said. "Take this money to your room and to-night, if he is sober, I'll send Bill Burgess up to your room. Give him the thousand dollars, but make him sign the receipt I've written out for you."

Abel again followed her to the head of the stairs. "What am I letting myself in for?" she thought.

As yet she had seen nothing of the town, so she turned up the street instead of going back to the hotel. She had just passed the stone bank building when she heard her name called, and stopped.

"Saw you pass the window, miss, and I wanted to talk to you," George A. Kump said. He was bareheaded, and somehow she didn't notice his ugliness quite as much as she had the day before.

"You—wanted to see me?" she faltered.

"Yes, won't you come in?"

She followed him into the bank. A little old man wearing spectacles was behind the grill.

"This is Miss Dixon, Barker," Kump called as they passed the cashier's window. "If she wants any cheques cashed you cash 'em."

He led the way into a small private office in the back and offered her a chair. "You're a nice looking girl with your face clean," he said.

"You didn't bring me in here just for that," she smiled.

"No. You worked in a bank before you came here, didn't you, Miss Dixon?"

"Yes, in Colorado."

"I need a bookkeeper mighty bad. How would you like to work for me as long as you stay in Highline?"

"Why, I—I don't know. I wanted a job, but I didn't expect——"

"How much was you gittin'?"

"Ninety dollars a month, but——"

"I'll give you a hundred. No, I'll make it a hundred and twenty. Probably costs more to live here."

"Mr. Kump, don't you think you would be taking a terrible

chance employing someone in your bank whose brother is accused of stealing from you?" she demanded.

"But I'm not hiring Willard," he pointed out smilingly. He rubbed his hand over his stiff grey hair and down over his red, bull neck in a gesture like a small boy's. She could see no guile in his ugly, kindly face.

"I'll take the job, Mr. Kump," she said, "and start work in the morning. But I want you to know that I wouldn't take it if I thought for a moment that my brother had stolen from you."

"Then it's a deal," he said enthusiastically, and engulfed her small hand in an enormous red paw.

CHAPTER VII "LOOK A-COMIN'"

THE BIG red barn and other outbuildings of the K Bar K ranch were quite commensurate with the power and influence of the owner in the county, but the ranchhouse itself might have been the domicile of any homesteader. Aside from the large kitchen and dining room, presided over by a half deaf old negro called Bilious, there were only three small rooms. One of these was reserved for George A. when he visited the ranch, which the old bachelor often did. That left a small sitting room, and a bedroom which Hondo occupied.

Hondo had eaten before he left town, so refused the supper the cook offered to get. He wasn't sleepy, but he didn't want to read so he played some records on his phonograph. Music sometimes helped him to think.

The whole Willard Dixon affair had been more of an irritation than anything else, up to now; although he had realized the implications if the kid was acquitted. The county was sparsely populated and George A. Kump's enemies would muster enough votes to elect Brig Dow sheriff, and the Thornberry outlaws would be protected in their lawlessness.

He knew that Kump could have saved himself by discharging him when he was accused by young Dixon, but George A. simply wasn't that kind of a man. Until recently it had seemed unthinkable that anybody would give credence to Willard's wild story, but now Hondo was seeing many averted faces whenever he went to town.

Ez and Rumel Thornberry with their attorney, Slick Abel, were backing Willard, not because they cared anything about the boy, but because they were fighting Hondo and his boss. Abel, he knew, was smart. The lawyer was probably trying to find out what lay in Hondo's past, and the thought of what he might find gave Hondo many an uneasy moment.

He didn't like courts and their ways. The Thornberrys were his enemies. They were men of violence, and that suited him. He knew how to deal with such as that. That was why, in anticipation of trouble over the wagon-loads of grain which Rumel Thornberry had practically confiscated from Bessie Bell, he had decided to take cattle up Swan Creek the next day.

He had about gone through his list of favourite records when there came a knock at the door. He swung about and started to call an invitation, but thought better of it. He swiftly transferred his sixgun from where it hung in its holster on the wall to his own lap. He was facing the door, but the gun was concealed when the door opened.

Pat Young stood there.

" Oh, come in, Pat," Hondo called.

Young, a naturally light-complexioned man with a tanned mahogany face, came across the carpet with a peculiar cat-like glide. He had a small scar across the flange of one nostril and his eyes were blue and hard, and unblinking.

" Heard your music-box, so thought I'd come in," he said in a low, soft voice.

" You ride late."

" Yeah." Young grinned slightly when Hondo got up and replaced his sixgun. " Connected with the decorations on your pan ? " he asked.

" More or less. Had to lick Rumel Thornberry today. Thought his brother might have decided to make a call about it."

" No, Ez has been quite busy. He's turned grain hauler."

" You don't tell me ! "

" I was projectin' around their place when I seen Ez start toward Esmeralda with some wagons and four horse teams, so I projected along behind. They met six wagons loaded with grain, and done some transferrin'. The other wagons headed back, an' I thought Thornberry would haul the grain home. Instead of that he headed into the hills."

" And you still projected along," Hondo said with a twinkle.

" Right. They finally dropped over a ridge and down an

old wood road into a canyon nearly five miles above their ranch. Darned if they ain't got a new log cabin built in there in the trees. I never would have found it if I hadn't been trailin' 'em. That's where they left their grain," Pat reported.

"O be joyful!" Hondo exulted. "Patrick, you're an angel!"

"That so?" Pat asked mildly. "I thought I was an ex-con."

"Anyway, you've knocked me out of a night's sleep, and the price of a pair of silk stockings. Grab yourself some sleep. I've got to go back to town."

Hondo started pounding on Bessie Bell's door just after midnight. He finally got Bessie to the other side of the closed door.

"Who is it?" she demanded suspiciously.

"It's Hondo. Open up, darling."

"For that I sure will," Bessie replied. "But wait till I get some clothes on."

She wore a bathrobe over her nightdress when she opened the door.

"I'd be scandalized forever if the neighbours saw me letting you in at this hour," she stated.

"You mean they'd be scandalized," he corrected. "You ain't sold them oats to Thornberry yet, have you?"

"I certainly ain't. You won't get out of buying those stockings that easily. I've already got a writ of replevin from Judge Tillman, and Ace Gillette is going out to serve it in the morning. What about it?"

"He can't serve the writ if he can't find the oats. And he can't find 'em."

"How do you know?"

"Because, darling, they didn't take those oats to their ranch." He told her then what Pat Young had seen.

"Why, the dirty thieves!" Bessie cried.

"Maybe it ain't so bad," Hondo said. "After they've had their fun with Gilette Ez is sure to show up with another offer of payment."

"Just what have you got on your mind, son?" Bessie asked curiously.

"I'll have them oats safely in a bin at the ranch before midnight to-morrow night. So, if Ez wants to donate some cash——"

"Whoa there! I don't want to get in bad by selling the same grain twice."

"You don't want to sell it to him. Just get mad and offer to bet him some money you actually get the grain back. Bet him any amount he wants, but be sure to make him put up the cash."

"I'd like to teach those thieves a lesson," Bessie said, "but how can I prove I've got the grain back?"

"There's several ways to do that," Hondo grinned. "First, you'll have my cheque on George A. in payment. Then, your drivers can identify the sacks. Finally, if he refuses to admit they are the same oats, tear up the writ of replevin, and offer to pay the debt and give him the oats if he can show 'em at his ranch in say five hours. But be sure to have the terms of the bet written down."

"All right, for the sake of the joke, and just to show those hoodlums they can't put anything over on me I will," Bessie promised.

Bessie made coffee and scrambled eggs and fried bacon. After they had eaten Hondo hurried back to the ranch, and arrived in time to rout out his crew even earlier than he had threatened.

He was really less concerned over Bessie's oats than with the other business of the day. The Thornberry ranch was located on the Swan Creek just inside a narrow arm of the main valley. Several miles above the ranch Swan Creek poured out of a narrow gorge where high, rocky shoulders pinched together, leaving only a narrow gateway to a wide, uneven, timbered covered watershed above that was called Swan Basin.

It had been K Bar K range for thirty years, for the K Bar K hay meadows were watered in part from Swan Creek before that stream plunged into Rock River twenty miles below. The past winter, however, the Thornberry brothers had issued an ultimatum that this range belonged to them and that any attempt upon the part of the K Bar K to use it would be resisted not only by the Thornberrys but by Brig Dow, and the whole colony of nesters.

This was the day Hondo had chosen to challenge that ultimatum.

They might be bluffing, and they might not. Hondo didn't know. He knew that George A. had told Ezra Thornberry, "You can have Swan Basin for your cattle, providing you sign an agreement to keep your stuff off the rest of my range."

Thornberry had refused.

All K Bar K cattle except a hundred and fifty head of weak stuff in the hospital bunch had been on the range now for some weeks. Hondo had been waiting for this bunch to get strong enough to drive. He had chosen these to put into Swan Basin because they could not be stampeded.

"We may be in for some trouble to-day, boys," he told the men when Bilious was serving their daybreak breakfast. "We're takin' the hospital bunch into Swan Basin, and you know what that means. Thornberry may try to stop us at the narrows."

"Why don't we git that fust ?" Spike Williams inquired.

"That's a darn good idea," Hondo agreed. "You an' Owen Denny take the long way and come down from above. Four more of us will drive the cattle up the ridge north of the creek. And Pat will take as many men and wagons as he needs to haul a little grain."

The Thornberrys had not taken the confiscated grain up the main road to their ranch. It was hidden in another canyon, well above their place. With the cattle in plain sight in the other direction there was not likely to be any of them bothering about the well-hidden grain.

It wasn't nine o'clock yet when the cattle came in sight of the Thornberry buildings on the other side of the creek. The little herd moved slowly along the side of an open ridge, at that point no more than two miles from the shabby log buildings standing back on a raised flat several hundred yards from the road.

It was fifteen minutes before Hondo saw signs of great activity. The Thornberrys had two hired riders, both as mean and tough as the men they worked for. One was a small, mean-eyed rat of a man named Lafe Lufkin, the other a great, none too bright, hulking fellow called Ozark, notorious for his cruelty to animals.

As the hospital bunch drifted slowly along, Hondo letting them take their time, two horsemen dashed down the road in the direction of Highline. Hondo was pretty certain they were not both going to town. Another rider took the road up the creek toward the ranch of a sixty-year-old nester named Gus Marks, who had been a thorn in the K Bar K flesh long before the advent of Ezra and Rumel Thornberry.

Hondo kept the little herd moving at the same easy gait. By this time Spike and Owen should have about reached the narrows, and that would prevent an ambush at the one logical place.

An hour and a half later Hondo bent the herd down off the ridge toward the creek bottom to enter the narrows. They were now out on a steep unprotected slope. He was hoping that his strategy had worked, and that there would be no trouble. Once he got inside the narrows there would be nothing to worry about, and if Ez Thornberry and Gus Marks had tried to get into the narrows he would have heard shots.

A shout from one of his own men, Nate Barstow, warned him he had congratulated himself too soon.

" Good God ! " Nate yelled, " Look a-comin' ! "

Hondo cast a startled glance upward in time to see a thin line of long, thin heads and horns just coming over the top of the ridge. He comprehended instantly, and not without dismay. At least two hundred head of wild Texas steers, which must have been hidden in some canyon for just this purpose, were sweeping down the side of the ridge in wild stampede, while behind, shooting and yelling like maniacs rode at least a dozen riders.

Once those wild steers struck the weak hospital bunch of Herefords complete hell would be let loose. The weaker cattle would be knocked down, killed or crippled. And a man would be risking his life to try to halt or turn that wicked stampede.

Never again, Hondo vowed, would he make the mistake of underestimating his enemies. Then, as a bullet struck a boulder just above him and ricochetted past his ear with an angry whine, he realized that he might not live to rectify his mistake.

CHAPTER VIII SOMERSAULTING LONGHORN

HONDO'S first thought was for his men. "Get out of the way!" he yelled at them, but promptly disobeyed his own advice as he spurred his horse desperately up the hill toward the oncoming avalanche of flesh, then raced along the upper side of his herd, until he reached the leaders.

He fired two shots so close that a bullet brought blood on the nose of a thin, red cow. The animal let out a startled, frenzied bawl, and turned in her tracks. So did the others.

Hondo crowded them hard. Had they been anything but the weak stuff they were, they would at least have struck a trot. But except for the maddened cow which was soon clear through the bunch, and leading the other way, their pace was no more than a fast walk.

Meanwhile, the longhorns were coming at express train speed. Although there were not more than two hundred of them their crackling hooves shook the mountainside. Hondo realized that if his strategy to deflect the stampede just enough that it would pass ahead of his own cows and calves failed then he would be caught directly in front of it, with no chance to escape.

The line of slobbering, snot-nosed steers came on like an avalanche. Their little red eyes were fixed in insane anger upon anything that interfered with their blind flight.

Hondo spurred desperately. He saw that he wasn't going to make it. He fired three times as fast as he could thumb the hammer. Two great, gaunt steers piled up. One of them with a bullet through its brain turned a complete somersault, and its tail swished the legs of Hondo's horse. But it was just enough to force the ones behind to veer away.

Had there been more of them the line would have held firm, but they were deflected just enough to miss Hondo's horse, but close enough that he could smell their grass-laden breath. They swept on down the sidehill, missing the other herd, except for one thin, lazy dogey. A steer struck it with his breast, bowled it over, and its agonized bellow rose just once above the clatter of split hooves on rock. When the stampede passed the dogey was no more than a still quivering mass of mangled flesh.

Hondo had just one cartridge left in his gun, and no time to reload. He didn't bother about the cattle. His eyes were upon the men. They drew their horses to a plunging halt around Hondo.

Rumel Thornberry was there, along with his two employees, Ozark and Lufkin, but he was not the spokesman. That honour fell to a burly rancher from Wild Dog Creek, several miles to the north. Brig Dow could call himself a rancher rather than a nester, and he could pass as a man of some education. He it was who was being groomed as Sheriff Watson's successor.

This bunch of miserable longhorns, Hondo knew, had been imported solely as an excuse to make trouble with the K Bar K. Dow had been ordered to keep them away from the K Bar K Herefords on penalty of having them shot, and he had wailed long and loudly from Highline to Esmeralda that this was another example of K Bar K tyranny.

Despite the man's bluster Hondo had long ago become convinced that he wasn't overburdened with nerve.

"You killed two of my steers," Dow bellowed. "By Gawd, I want pay for 'em. Right now."

Hondo merely looked the man over coldly. In the oppressive silence Rumel piped up in his high, shrill voice, "And then take yore damn' dogeys back where they belong. This is our range."

Hondo's three men were now but a few yards away. It wasn't much of a fighting crew, for his real fighting men were elsewhere. But at least he wasn't alone.

"Turn the herd back the other way now, Nate, and head for the narrows," he called out. "As for paying you anything, Dow, I'd see you in hell first."

He had holstered his gun, but his foes had not. He kept his eyes upon two men—Thornberry and Dow.

"You—you got a hell of a nerve," Dow mouthed.

"Nerve enough that I can get you and Rumel before your apes here can get me," Hondo challenged coldly. They couldn't know that he had but one cartridge left. They couldn't know which one he would try to get first.

Brig Dow was first to break the long silence. "Two steers ain't worth killin' a man for, but I'll sue you for 'em," he threatened.

Hondo turned his horse a little so that he faced the entire group. Nate and the others now had the hospital herd turned toward the narrows, all except the nose-wounded cow which had already reached the creek. Hondo sat there and waited. The next move was up to them.

They sensed that if they tried to turn the herd back Hondo would start shooting, despite the odds; and they couldn't make up their minds. The little herd passed as if in review. The longhorns had now scattered beyond the creek and stopped running.

It was a tense moment. If trouble started Hondo meant to use his one bullet on Rumel Thornberry, and believed the man sensed it.

"Come on, fellers," Rumel said at last. "We'll just wait at the narrows, and make damn' sure nothin' goes through there."

"Just a minute," Hondo called crisply. "You didn't think I was fool enough to come in here with only three men, did you? The rest of my crew has been waiting there in the narrows for hours. You mess around down there and you'll get hurt."

They rode away, and Hondo fell in behind the cattle.

"My lord, Hondo, I won't git over the scare I got when I saw you pinned in between them two bunches of cattle, till old Gabe toots his horn," Nate Barstow remarked.

Hondo smiled. He saw that all three were still white and shaking.

The Swan Creek men angled toward the narrows, but before they reached the creek they turned off and once across they began to gather up the longhorns. They had sighted Spike Williams and Owen Denny, and they had no reason to suppose that they were not backed up by a dozen more men.

It wasn't long past noon when Hondo's crew got through the narrows, and allowed the tired convalescents to spread out and graze.

"I don't believe they'll be bothered now," Hondo said. "Those fellows ought to have sense enough to know that we could make it tougher on them than they can on us."

"I reckon all they really want is an excuse to howl about how the K Bar K runs it over the little feller," Spike said with undeniable wisdon.

"The rest of you stick here a few hours," Hondo said.

"I'm curious to know how Pat and Ben and the boys are coming on. Owen, you better come with me."

They returned by the wood road on the south side of the creek, a road that ran between the Thornberry buildings and their hay land.

By that time the longhorns were being held in a bunch not far from the creek and directly below where old Gus Marks lived. As Hondo and nineteen-year-old Owen Denny crossed the creek three men rode to intercept them. Brig Dow, the owner of the longhorns, was one, but the other two had not been present on the ridge. They were Ez Thornberry and Gus Marks.

Although Ez Thornberry was five years older than his brother they looked much alike. Ez was stooped, and more gaunt, and paid less attention to his personal appearance. Both men were bachelors, as was Marks. They reached the road a little ahead of Hondo and Owen and waited.

"Now you got your damn' cattle in Swan Basin I suppose you'll object to me grazin' mine in there on government land at all," Ez Thornberry said as Hondo stopped.

"I'd a hell of a lot rather you didn't," Hondo said frankly, "but we've never tried to hog the range like you fellows. Turn 'em in if you want, but leave our stuff alone."

"You talk nice, but I notice you always feed off the range close to us first, so when fall comes our stuff are scattered from hell to breakfast," Ez Thornberry said bitterly.

"Your own fault. George A. has offered to divide the range with you."

"On his terms. But there'll be a new deal after the election next fall when we git a sheriff who'll defend our rights," Ez said.

"Meaning Brig here, I suppose. I don't think I'll vote for him."

"You won't vote for anybody, you crook, because you'll be in the pen," Ez broke out.

"Bankin' pretty heavy on that frame-up, ain't you, Ez?" Hondo retorted. "Such things have a way of back-firin' sometimes."

"You're not takin' to Rumel now," Ez growled. "I don't bluff like he does."

"I may try you out some time," Hondo said easily. "All I've got to say to you now is don't bother those cattle up in the basin."

Gus Marks said, " Take my advice, Hondo, an' leave this country. You can't admire yourself on a marble slab, yuh know."

Hondo turned slowly and surveyed the old man grimly. Marks' pale eyes didn't falter. He was a wicked old man, and a known thief, but he had never been known as a gunman. Somehow Hondo got the impression that the warning was sincere.

Hondo changed his mind about investigating the grain hauling business. There was too much danger of being followed.

Near the mouth of the canyon he met young Deputy Sheriff Ace Gillette.

" Hello, what're you doin' up here ? " Ace inquired.

" Just been takin' a bunch of weak stuff into Swan Basin," Hondo replied innocently.

" I see. Was afraid you might have been tryin' to locate Bessie's oats. I wouldn't be courtin' trouble with the Thornberrys if I was you—not the way the roads are."

" You mean while I'm under suspicion of stealin' cattle from my own outfit."

" That's right. Understand, I don't believe a damn' word of it, but you'd be wise to keep your nose clean. Sheriff Watson kinda leans the other way, even though it means his job if they uphold the Dixon kid."

Hondo felt more concern than he showed. " That so ? What's been eatin' the sheriff ? " he inquired.

" I think it's something he's found out," Ace said.

Hondo got the impression that had it not been for Owen being along the deputy would have said more. Before getting to be deputy Ace had been a rider for the K Bar K.

" I suppose you've got that writ of replevin' for Bessie," Hondo remarked.

" Yep. She got it from Judge Tillman. If I can find the grain I'll attach it."

" Think you'll find it ? "

" I ain't sure. They might have hauled it to somebody else's place—Brig Dow's likely. If they did it may be hard to prove it's exactly the same oats."

" Yeah, I guess it would."

It was nearly midnight when Hondo, working on the ranch books, heard the rumble of wagons in the yard. Going out he saw his big wagons, each drawn by a four-horse team, lined up near the granary. Pat Young, on horseback, came to meet him.

"Well, you got it," Hondo said. "Any trouble?"

"Not a bit," Pat answered. "We loaded up right after daybreak, and pulled down the canyon a couple of miles, rolled in behind an aspen grove and waited till after dark to come on home. Never saw a soul. But we took time to drive a big bunch of cattle over all our tracks. Nobody could ever prove we brought the stuff here."

"All right, unload it, and put the hay-racks back on the wagons," Hondo directed. "Bilious will have supper ready by that time."

All in all, Hondo thought, it had been a bad day for the Thornberrys.

CHAPTER XI — THE BRIBE

NO SOONER was Daphne out of the bank than she wondered if she was being disloyal to Willard by hiring out to George A. Kump. She dismissed the thought quickly. After all, she had borrowed five hundred dollars which had to be paid back, and the quicker she got to work the better.

Besides, she thought, if she could make the ugly old man like her she might get him to see that there was no more reason to suppose Willard would steal from him than would Hondo Horn.

She felt uncomfortable with that thousand dollars in her knitted handbag. What if she should be robbed, or lose it? She clutched it tightly when she went into the hotel, and felt increasingly nervous when Nick Cropopolos engaged her in trifling conversation. Nick wanted to know if she played chess.

"I'm sorry, but a simple game of checkers is all I can manage," she said.

"Why, that's fine," he said. "You come down some time and we have a game. I like to play poker, but in a poker game I'm only the Greek who comes bearing gifts."

Daphne laughed. "I hear you should beware of them," she said.

They were still talking when the young prosecuting attorney entered the hotel. He stared nearsightedly at Daphne, bowed gravely and lifted his hat But he passed on.

"That Harol' he nice boy, but take himself too damn much serious," Nick volunteered.

That was plain to see. His frigid attitude seemed designed as a warning to Daphne not to try any feminine wiles on him. As if she would, she thought resentfully.

"Does Mr. Thatcher room here?" she asked.

"Just across the hall from you," Nick beamed.

Daphne felt ill. In a few hours she was going to be visited by a man to whom she was going to pay money, and she wasn't sure whether it was to get him to tell the truth or to tell a lie. She knew there was a thing called subornation of perjury. What would happen if Thatcher happened to see Burgess entering or leaving her room?

Willard's defeatist attitude was the thing that puzzled her. She forced herself to believe in his innocence. So, if he was innocent, Hondo Horn had given him the money, and there could be nothing wrong in finding a corroborative witness.

Nevertheless, she felt like a guilty conspirator when, sometime between ten and eleven o'clock there came a furtive knock on her door. She crossed quickly and opened it. A short old man, holding a little round hat in his hand, stood there smirking and grinning. Because of a mat of tangled white whiskers she could see little of his face except a red blob of a nose, and small, watery eyes, remote and greedy. A round bit of pink bald head shone above a fringe of hair that looked white on top, and yellow at the roots.

"Come in," she said hastily.

The old man bobbed, and stepped through with unexpectedly alert steps. Daphne closed the door, then prompted by impulse opened it a crack to see if anyone was watching. There was no one in sight.

"You are—Mr. Burgess?" she asked.

"That's me, Bill Burgess," the old man replied in a whisky-harsh voice. He was grinning, but his grin didn't seem particularly amiable.

"Have a seat, Mr. Burgess," she invited. "I suppose Attorney Abel sent you up here?"

"That's right."

"Does—does anyone else know you are up here?"

"Not a soul, ma'am. Not even Nick Cropopolos saw me come up."

"I want to ask you some questions, Mr. Burgess. How well do you know my brother?"

"Purty well, ma'am. He was a good-hearted boy. Never come to town he didn't buy me a drink." He didn't add that he always tried to cadge a drink from every possible prospect.

"You know Hondo Horn, of course?"

"Naturally. Who don't around here. Old fellers like me know enough to keep away from him."

"You mean, he abuses you."

"Ma'am, I've had Hondo Horn almost knock my head off, just because he didn't like me near him at the bar. I've seen him threaten to kill a man just for steppin' on his foot accidental."

"Humph! Now Mr. Burgess, is it true that you saw Hondo Horn pay my brother some money and heard him tell Willard to buy hay with it?"

"Ma'am, it's as true as the Holy Book itself."

"Willard says you didn't see it," she shot out.

The old bar-fly was unperturbed. "He don't say he didn't git the money, does he?" he asked.

"No-o, he says he did."

"Well, I reckon he didn't see me, but I saw him. It was this way, ma'am. I hate to confess it, but on that day I'd had jest a *mite* too much to drink. I went into the back room of the Senate to lay down. I crawled in behind some old chairs they've got back there, and after a while the bartender come back and covered me with an old piece of carpet.

"When I woke up I was too stiff an' sick to move. It was voices woke me up, and there was two men almost on top of me. It was Hondo Horn and your brother. I remember Hondo had one foot up on a chair."

Burgess paused as if to give this circumstantial detail time to sink in. Then he resumed.

First, I couldn't tell what they were talkin' about. It sounded like Hondo was tryin' to persuade your brother to do something he didn't want to do. Then I heard your brother say, 'Why don't you buy the hay? I hate to be responsible for so much cash.'"

"Then what did Hondo say?" Daphne breathed.

"He went on to say that he was too busy to see Sep Kohler. Said if they wasn't short on hay at the ranch that he'd drive the cattle down. Finally, I see him pull out his wallet and count out a wad of money. I didn't see how much, but Hondo said if Willard could buy the hay any cheaper he could keep the difference."

Daphne got up and paced the room. She couldn't doubt that the old man was telling the truth, and her heart swelled with bitterness against Hondo Horn. At that moment she was more concerned in bringing him to justice than in saving Willard.

"You say they didn't see you?" she asked.

"I made blame well certain they didn't," Burgess stated. "Hondo Horn would've stomped me through the floor if he'd guessed I was eavesdroppin' on him."

"If this is true then why are you reluctant about going on the witness stand and telling what you saw?" she asked bluntly. "Why do you have to be bribed?"

Burgess twisted his little round hat in his hands. "Bribed is a hard word, ma'am," he whined. "I don't call it that. I'm a poor, lonely old man. I can't work hard any more. Here I have some friends who look out fer me. But if I told that story Hondo Horn or some of his men would do fer me right enough. I'd have to go 'way. Ma'am, what could a helpless old man do alone among strangers without money? Go to the poorhouse, that's what he'd have to do. That's what yo're askin'. Yo're askin' me to go to the poorhouse or mebbe git beat up or killed to save your brother."

He stood up, and he was actually weeping. He brushed a shiny sleeve across his eyes to wipe away the tears as he stumbled toward the door.

"Wait," Daphne cried. "How much would you have to have?"

Burgess paused with his hand on the door-knob. "Slick Abel said you would pay me a thousand. It's not too much."

"How do I know you would stick to your story if I gave you the money?"

"I'll go right over to Slick Abel's office an' sign an affydavit," the old man vowed. "An' you have my word of honour."

"I'll give you the money," she decided suddenly, "because I think you are telling the truth. But only on condition you put the money in the bank, or let somebody like Mr. Abel handle it. I don't want you to be broke when the trial comes up."

"Your distrust grieves me deeply, ma'am. Putting the money in George Kump's bank would give rise to talk. It might discredit my story, and even land you in jail. As for Slick Abel, no ma'am. I can trust myself further than I kin him. No thousand dollars, no testimony."

Whisky-sodden as he was he knew when he had the whip-hand. With great reluctance Daphne went to her handbag and counted out the money. Burgess counted it over after her, and thrust it into the inside pocket of his tattered coat.

She opened the door, made sure that the hall was vacant, and sent him on his way. She watched uneasily until the little round hat made its final bob out of sight on the stairway. She continued to have the feeling that she had done a very foolish thing.

Daphne was ready for work at nine the next morning. Barker, the cashier, greeted her coldly—he was not pleased at having a woman assistant—but George A. Kump shouted a hearty, "Good-morning, Daphne."

She took off her coat and went to work, but she was eager for the noon hour. Instead of going back to Nick's for lunch she darted up the stairway beside the drugstore and into Aaron Abel's law office.

"Ah, Miss Dixon, I was expecting you," the lawyer greeted. "How do you like your new job?"

"It's all right. I must say Mr. Kump is nice to work for. Have you—have you seen Mr. Bill Burgess?"

"Oh, yes. You see I was waiting for him when he came from your room last night, and I brought him right up here."

"Oh!"

"I've got his deposition—just in case anything should happen to him. Here it is. I think you should keep it."

"I?"

"For this reason. With you it will be safe. It's not beyond Hondo Horn to take over this office with his ruffians and destroy everything if he suspected such a document was here."

She glanced at the deposition, and saw that it contained approximately the same story Burgess had told her the evening before. She put it into her handbag, with the feeling that there were safer places than that.

"What about the money? Isn't there danger he will drink it up before the trial?" she asked.

"Not a bit," Abel laughed. "You see I was not alone. Burgess didn't like it a bit, but we took the money away from him. I told him it would be his just as soon as his testimony was given, not before."

Daphne was beginning to understand how the lawyer had gained his nickname, " Slick."

" Will you do another favour for me, Mr. Abel ? " she asked. " I won't get off work until four or five o'clock. Could you arrange to see the sheriff about letting me visit Willard at five o'clock ? "

" I'll try," Abel promised. " But remember, the sheriff is no friend of mine."

She started back to work without her lunch. She had not quite reached the bank steps when two horsemen turned the corner and stopped. One was Hondo Horn ; the other a smaller, slimmer, older man with a hard, reckless face, slightly belied by twinkling blue eyes, which could yet turn diamond hard on a moment's notice. This was Pat Young, and Daphne would not noticed him at all, except for a certain wary manner in which he seemed to look in all directions without appearing to be more than mildly curious.

It was Hondo Horn who took her eye. Since her talk with Bill Burgess she had been more than ever convinced that he was an unmitigated scoundrel. And yet there was something electric in his gaze which lighted flames inside her brain when he turned his eyes upon her.

" Miss Dixon ! " he said softly, touching his hand briefly to the brim of his hat. She didn't know whether it was a greeting or an exclamation. But she did know that she wasn't going to speak to him—except on business.

Face flaming red, and rounded chin held high, she turned her back upon the two men and entered the bank. Even then she had a swift vision of Pat Young turning raised, mocking eyebrows upon his friend and foreman.

" Well, back early ain't you, Daphne ? " Kump queried.

" Am I ? " she asked. Then to cover her confusion added, " Don't you ever go out to eat, Mr. Kump ? "

" Generally have a lunch sent in," he replied. " Got one here now. If you git hungry help yourself. I think I'll go over to Nick's after all."

She flushed with embarrassment. He had been telling her that he knew she hadn't eaten. She would have starved before touching his lunch.

She hung up her hat and jacket, and seated herself at a desk near the end of the open hallway that ran from the main office of the bank to the private office of Mr. Kump at the rear. Barker was out to lunch, too, and Mr. Kump was at the grill.

The two punchers had followed her into the bank, but she refused to raise her eyes.

" Hello, Hondo, what brings you in here ? " Kump asked.

" Got a minute for a private talk ? " Hondo asked.

" Sure. Daphne, hold down the window till Barker comes back, will you ? " Kump strode past her into his private office, and Daphne stepped over to the grill. A few minutes later Barker came in with his manner of breathless importance, as though the future of the bank was in his hands, and Daphne returned to her desk. To her surprise and satisfaction she could hear every word spoken by the men in the private office. They were just out of sight, but far from out of hearing since there was no partition past the end of the hallway.

" I don't like it, boys," she heard Kump saying. " That kind of stuff is liable to land you both in the penitentiary."

Hondo Horn plunged even lower in Daphne's estimation when she heard him answer, " I don't know. I thought it was a real neat frame-up on the Thornberrys."

Chapter X — Beaten with Bridle Chains

Hondo had reported the oat business to his employer. As Daphne had overheard, George A. Kump was not enthusiastic about it.

" All right," he had said, " go ahead and make out your draft. I'll honour it."

Hondo and Pat soon arose to go. " By the way," Hondo said, " I got the hospital bunch up in Swan Basin yesterday."

" Any trouble ? " Kump asked suspiciously.

" Not to any extent. Brig Dow and a bunch of Thornberry's friends tried to stampede a bunch of Dow's Texas longhorns through us and I had to shoot a couple."

" All right," George A. said, " I'll back you up in anything you do."

They left through the lobby then, leaving Daphne uncertain whether Hondo had shot a couple of steers or a couple of men. But she did know that he was an unprincipled desperado, and that his boss, and hers, would back him up in his lawlessness.

Hondo looked over the low partition and saw Daphne bowed at her desk. She knew he was looking at her, but she didn't look up.

" I sort of gleaned the idee that that girl in there don't like you much, Hondo," Pat said when they were outside.

" She may not," Hondo said dubiously. " I may have some rough ploughin' there."

" What do you mean ? "

" Ever fall in love with a photograph, Pat ? "

" Hell, no."

" I did. That's what I mean."

While Pat was still puzzling the remark they met Sheriff John Watson. The sheriff stopped them. While his remarks were all addressed to Hondo his eyes dwelt almost constantly upon Pat.

" I hear you had some trouble out there yesterday, Hondo," he said.

" Who was telling you that, Sheriff ? "

" Brig Dow. Claims you killed two of his steers, and kept him from getting his herd into Swan Basin. That's government land, you know, Hondo."

" Look, Sheriff : The shoe was on the other foot. They tried to stop us. They stampeded them longhorns to do up the bunch of weak stuff we were driving. I shot two steers to turn the stampede. I'll argue the case with Dow in any manner he wants to name."

" I don't doubt you're right," the sheriff said almost apologetically, " but I've got to investigate. You know Brig Dow wants my office."

" You want me to plead guilty so you can save some votes?"

" Don't go flyin' off the handle with me, Hondo," the sheriff said patiently. " You're in pretty bad as it is, and you need my friendship. If a jury finds that Dixon kid not guilty you know what to expect. Who's your friend ? "

" Pat Young. We started riding together when we were kids. Known each other for a long time," Hondo said curtly.

" I see. Thought his face looked familiar."

The sheriff passed on.

" Well, Hondo, looks like it's time for Patrick to roll his soogans," Pat said.

" Why ? " Hondo demanded. " Nobody's got anything on you. I got troubles, too, but I'm not running from 'em."

Pat said nothing, and they entered a saloon.

They drank sparingly, leaning against one end of the bar and talking in low tones. No one approached them. Hondo had been well liked in Highline, but never popular in the usual sense of the term. He had minded his own business, but had never gone out of his way to be a hail-fellow-well-met. His friends were usually the more quiet people. His enemies the toughs and rowdies

Occasionally now someone came in and spoke to him. Hondo's greeting was friendly, but not effusive, and no one stopped to join them.

They had deliberately left their horses in front of the bank. Hondo was not taken altogether by surprise when the two Thornberrys, their two employees, Ozark, and Lafe Lufkin, and half a dozen of their friends barged into the saloon. But the other crowd was not expecting to find him at the bar.

" Looks like trouble," Pat murmured as the group stopped just inside the door for a whispered conference.

Brig Dow was among the group. As an aspirant to the office of sheriff he was not likely to become embroiled in a row. He was doing most of the talking now.

The bunch of them advanced upon the bar ; Ez and Rumel Thornberry on the flank next to Hondo and Pat, with Brig Dow next to them.

"What'll you have, gents?" the worried barkeeper inquired.

" Whisky," Ez Thornberry roared. " For everybody from here up." He had very pointedly not included the two men already at the end of the bar, although two or three men who had been drinking there were included.

As the bartender started to set out glasses Hondo and Pat replaced their beer glasses on the bar and started to leave.

" Just a minute, Horn," Ez Thornberry said loudly. " Got a little matter o' business to discuss with you."

" I didn't know we had any business, Thornberry."

" I think you did. I'm givin' you till just dark to-night to haul them oats back."

" What oats ? " Hondo queried gently.

" You know what oats," the man's voice rose angrily. " The oats you stole from our new salt cabin."

" I'm afraid you're barkin' up the wrong tree, as usual,

Thornberry. I've stolen no oats from you or anybody else." Hondo started away, but Ez Thornberry seized his lapel. Hondo swung about, and his grey eyes narrowed dangerously.

"Never do that," he almost whispered, and Thornberry let go.

"This is one time you overreached yoreself, Horn," the man said. "You see, we been talkin' to one o' yore punchers, an' he told us all about you sendin' wagons on to private land in the night an' haulin' them oats away."

Hondo missed the main implication. "Private land?" he said. "What and whose private land?"

"Mine," Lafe Lufkin piped up. "The cabin where that grain was stored was on my homestead."

Hondo was momentarily disconcerted. He wasn't sure whether that would have legal consequences or not. He had certainly never dreamed that anyone would have a homestead up there, and he still thought they were bluffing.

"It was a nice stunt, puttin' Bess Bell up to makin' a five hundred dollar bet with Ez that she'd git the oats back, an' then you stealin' 'em, but it won't work," Rumel put in.

"If there's any question of stealing then you're the boys to look out," Hondo said quietly. "You did steal that grain from Bessie. If she got it back she had the law behind her. Ask Ace Gillette."

"Listen, Horn!" Ez roared, "you can't steal what you pay for. We offered that woman a cheque, and it's still posted with our attorney. We want them oats back. If they ain't back by dark we're comin' after 'em."

"That'll be just dandy," Hondo said.

Hondo started on, then stopped. "You said you were talking to one of my men. Who was it?"

"You'll know when you see him," Ez Thornberry said.

"I've got a feeling, Thornberry, that I'm going to have to kill you one of these times," Hondo said deliberately, ignoring Pat Young's tug at his sleeve.

"But not to-day, Hondo," came Sheriff Watson's voice from the front door. "This party is breakin' up."

Lufkin, Ozark, and one or two others as well as Rumel Thornberry had their hands on their guns, but they hesitated.

"Shoot the first one that makes an awkward move on either side, Ace," the sheriff said.

The Thornberry clan jerked their heads around and saw Ace Gillette just inside the back door.

Hondo and Pat didn't look around. They started toward the front door.

"I don't like the kind of shows you put on, Sheriff," Hondo told Watson as he passed. "When the time comes for a showdown with them crooks it'll come off whether you're around or whether you ain't."

"I may not be much of a sheriff, Hondo, but as long as I hold the job I mean to keep order," the grey-moustached officer retorted coldly.

The two friends were untying their horses when George A. came out of the bank. The old cattleman looked anxious.

"The Thornberrys are in," he said. "You had any trouble?"

"Not yet. They claim they're coming after that grain if we don't haul it back," Hondo responded.

The old man passed his huge hand over his homely face, and caressed his red neck in a characteristic gesture.

"Let 'em come," he rumbled. "I'm about fed up, too. I'll be out to the ranch to-night."

"Don't worry, they'll not show up," Hondo said.

They mounted and rode to the feed store. Bessie, an anxious expression on her face, awaited them.

"I'm going to call that bet off, Hondo," she said. "I'll let old Ez keep his five hundred dollars. I wish I'd let him keep the grain."

"I don't," Hondo said. "This is a free country. A man don't have to sell anybody anything if he don't want to."

"But there'll be trouble, Hondo."

"Of course. Rumel taking that grain from your drivers wasn't just to get a few oats. Can't you see that? Everything the Thornberrys do has a purpose. It all fits into a pattern—a pattern woven for 'em by a smart crook named Slick Abel."

"It's too deep for me. I only know I'm afraid something will happen to you," Bessie said honestly.

"Everything they do is designed to look like George A. Kump is running the country and making it tough on the smaller fellows—like them. They're making Sheriff Watson look like an inefficient old goat. They think when they get me behind bars everything can be settled their way at the ballot box. But I've got another idea."

"I don't like the mood you're in, Hondo," Bessie said flatly. "They want to trick you into starting something, and like a fool I've played into their hands."

"The grain business is settled. All you've got to do is cash my draft at the bank, and collect your bet. But there is some unfinished business."

" Don't crowd 'em, Hondo."

" Would you say that if you knew they had murdered your husband ? " Hondo asked.

" Hunh ? What did you say ? " Bessie gasped.

" Tim Bell was my friend," Hondo said. " Other people may believe he was accidentally shot by some greenhorn deer-hunter like they claim, but I don't believe it, and I never have."

" Have you got any evidence at all ? " Bessie asked.

They were inside the office now, and Pat Young stood in the doorway looking at them with half amused, half cynical interest.

" No," Hondo said shortly. " Nothing that would hold good in a court."

"Come clean, Hondo," Bessie ordered. "As Tim's widow I'm slightly interested, you know. What're you holding back ? "

" A lie," he replied gravely. " Just a lie—maybe a couple of 'em."

Bessie seated herself behind her desk, waiting. Her plump cheeks had gone a little white. " Who do you think did it ? " she inquired.

" I don't know. I don't want to stir you up, Bessie, but I've never thought Tim was killed accidentally, although it does happen sometimes. When we find out who did it I think that like all the other things that have happened it'll tie up."

" I see," Bessie said slowly. " I think I see what you mean. But it's all the more important you don't let them prod you into something."

They went out, with Pat Young looking more puzzled than ever. " I don't get it," he said finally. " Who the hell do you think murdered Bell—if he was murdered ? "

" Let's wait till to-morrow. Maybe we'll find out."

It was sundown when they got back to the ranch. They unsaddled and turned their mounts loose to roll, then went directly to the bunkhouse. Most of the men were in. They watched Hondo uneasily without speaking. He glanced swiftly over the interior of the long log room, then walked directly over to where someone lay on a bunk with his face toward the wall.

" Turn over, Owen," he said grimly, " and tell me how it happened."

The boy in the bunk uttered a choking sob, but didn't move.

" He can't very well, Hondo," old Ben Rambeau spoke up. " They riddled his back. We bandaged him up as good as we could."

" Looks like they used bridle reins—the chain ends," Spike Williams offered.

" I didn't want to tell 'em anything. I tried not to," the young puncher cried. " I guess I fainted once. When I come to they started in again, an' I couldn't stand it. I had to tell 'em it was our wagons got that grain, but I didn't mention any names."

Hondo and Pat exchanged glances.

" It's all right, Owen," Hondo said. " You ought to have told 'em before they did all that to you." He leaned over and saw that the boy's face had been beaten, too. " You take it easy till you get well. Your pay will go on just the same. Who was in the party ? "

" Both Thornberrys. It was Ez done most of the whippin' —him an' Ozark. Lafe Lufkin, Heb Giles, an' Walk Turgood was there, too. They jumped me before I knew they was around," Owen explained feebly.

The two he last mentioned were a pair of unsavoury nesters who were usually fawning at the heels of Brig Dow and the Thornberrys.

Hondo withdrew. " Better go fetch Doc Beck," he told Spike Williams. " He may be hurt worse than we think."

Pat Young had followed him outside. " That kid is a hell of a lot grittier than some of them skunks up the creek are," he said meaningly.

" Just what I was thinking, Pat," Hondo replied grimly. " Just what I was thinking."

CHAPTER XI HANGED BY A THUMB

THAT had been a hectic day at the Hghline State Bank. Daphne was still tingling with indignation as a result of what she had overheard Hondo Horn say when the sheriff came in. He, too, passed into the little semi-private office at the back. Daphne listened attentively.

" Just saw Hondo," the sheriff said.

" Yes, he just left here."

" Who was the waddy with him ? "

" Name's Pat Young. Old friend of Hondo's. Good man, I hear."

The sheriff's next words made Daphne fairly jump.

" George A.," Watson inquired grimly, " did you ever know that Hondo Horn had served time ? "

After Daphne's first startled gasp she held her breath waiting for the banker's reply. It was slow in coming, but his voice was calm and even when he did reply.

" Yes, John, I know all about it. Hondo told me the whole story when I asked him to be my foreman, and I took the trouble to find out if he was telling the truth. He was convicted of helping to rob a bank, but he only served about six months when he was pardoned. The real bandit voluntarily came forward and confessed the crime."

" That's about the way I got it. Remember the real thief's name ? "

" No. Why ? "

" I dunno. His name wasn't Pat Young, but I saw the picture of the fellow and it looked a lot like this bird Young. And if Young ain't an ex-con then I never saw one."

Daphne heard her employer get up. She knew that he had forgotten all about her presence.

" The implication is that if it comes out people will think Hondo was in with him on the job, and that Young just took the rap. Is that it ? " Kump asked angrily.

" It won't look good for Hondo when the Dixon case comes on for trial."

" The Dixon—case."

Daphne knew then that Kump had just remembered her

presence. At that moment he was probably regretting having offered her a job.

" I don't give a damn what it looks like, John, I'm backing Hondo to the limit," Kump declared positively.

" And it's my duty to find out all the facts in the case I can," the sheriff said.

" And yet people have the audacity to say that you take orders from me," Kump said bitterly.

" I reckon I do owe my election to your support, and now it looks like I'll lose it. But while I'm sheriff I do my duty as I see it," Watson said.

" And that's why Slick Abel and his outfit mean to throw you out of office," Kump said. " Well, John, there's no hard feelin's. We both belong to the old school, so we know where we stand."

Daphne regarded the stoop-shouldered old sheriff with new interest as he shuffled out. Despite what Abel had said she no longer regarded him as an enemy.

George A. Kump didn't come out from his office, and presently he had another visitor. This time it was Bessie Bell.

Bessie inquired for Kump at the window, and Barker told her to go on into the office. As she passed, Bessie looked over at Daphne and called, " Hello there, how's it going ? "

" Fine," Daphne replied. " Just fine."

The girl hated to listen in to this conversation, too, but if she stayed at her desk she couldn't help overhearing, and she had no excuse to leave.

She heard them exchange amenities, then Bessie said, " I've got Hondo's draft here for the price of some oats. I don't know whether to cash it or not."

" There's no reason on earth why not, Bessie. It was your grain, and you've got a right to sell it where you want. Just tell Barker to credit it to your account. Nothing else was there, Bessie ? "

Daphne guessed that Kump was warning Bessie about her.

" No—o," Bessie said. " I guess not. Yes, there is, too. George A., I heard a man say to-day that he didn't think my husband was shot accidentally. It—it was something of a shock."

" Tim didn't have any enemies, did he ? "

" Not many. But he was lucky at gambling. He was a fiend for it, and although I know he was a square gambler he was so lucky that lots of people thought he was crooked."

"He cleaned the Thornberrys a few times, didn't he?"

"Yes, and they did Tim some dirty tricks. That's one reason I've always refused to sell them anything. That and the way they've tried to run over Hondo."

"I'm worried, too, Bessie," Kump confessed. "I'm an old man. I built my business on the square, and when I had enemies I fought it out with 'em on the square. I can fight wolves, but I guess my eyesight is too poor to fight off snakes. I'm beginning to feel beaten."

"Don't feel that way, George A., just because I do. I'm only a woman. I'm sorry I bothered you with my troubles. Good-bye."

Bessie didn't look toward Daphne as she went out. A moment later the old man entered the main office of the bank. Daphne noticed that his tread was heavy, although he was physically tired.

"You better run along now, Miss Dixon," he said. "I almost forgot. To-morrow's Sunday. May find it dull in Highline. If you want to take a ride I keep a gentle mare over in Bessie's livery stable. You're welcome to use her."

He was kind. Daphne could not have blamed him at all had he told her he didn't need her any more. She almost wished she hadn't heard anything at the bank, but for Willard's sake she had information that had to be imparted to Mr. Abel.

She went immediately to the lawyer's office. His greeting was considerably more informal than usual.

"Hello, Daphne, my dear," he said, "come right in. How's the work?"

"It's not difficult," she said stiffly. "I won't sit. I want to see Willard right away."

"Anything on your mind?"

Hurriedly she told him about Hondo's visit to the bank, and then the sheriff's. Abel's eyes grew brighter as she talked.

"So friend Hondo is a jailbird!" he exclaimed. "That won't hurt your brother's case at all when I get Horn on the witness stand."

"I wish the trial was over," she said.

"It soon will be," he said. "The defence is ready. We go to trial in a couple of days."

"So soon? I thought it would be much longer."

"No, I was going to ask for an extension, but instead I'll tell the judge we are ready."

"I'm glad of that," Daphne said.

She found Ace Gillette, the good-looking young deputy, on duty at the courthouse. He acceded readily to her request to see Willard.

Her brother was in a better mood this time, and asked her how she liked her job.

" It's not at all difficult, but it makes me feel like a spy," she said. " However, I found out something to-day that will help our case."

" What's that ? "

" Hondo Horn is an ex-convict. He was pardoned, but now it seems like he might have been guilty after all. When we prove that, the jury is sure to believe he was the thief and not you."

Willard remained silent.

" But that's not the best news I've got. That witness who saw Hondo give you the money is going to testify."

" I told you Bill Burgess nor nobody else saw Hondo give give me any money," he said angrily.

" But he *did*, Willard. You just happened not to see him. He was in the back room of that saloon, and overheard everything that was said. Look : Here's his deposition, in case anything happens to him."

Willard took the deposition and read it with an air of incredulity.

" How much did you pay him to swear to this ? ' he asked cynically.

" A thousand dollars. I had to. Oh, Willard, I don't mind the money. Clearing your name is all I care about."

" Well," he said sardonically, " it don't look like Slick Abel has missed any bets."

" Willard, you act like you hated your attorney ! He's doing the very best he can to get you acquitted."

He sullenly rolled a cigarette. Plainly he wanted her to go.

" I can't understand you, Willard," she said, on the verge of tears. " You claim Hondo Horn gave you that money in the back room of the Senate Saloon, and yet you seem to be angry because there is a witness to prove your story."

" Oh, shut up, and get to hell out of here," he cried rudely.

Hurt more deeply, perhaps, than she had ever been in her life, Daphne stepped to the door of the cell and motioned blindly for Ace Gillette to let her out.

She didn't sleep much that night, and she dreaded the long,

inactive day that lay ahead. She couldn't bring herself to see Willard again so soon.

Then she remembered George A's offer to lend her a horse. She liked to ride, and it would be a blessed relief to get away from everything for a while. As soon as she had made a pretence of eating breakfast she put on her hat and coat and hurried down to the Bell livery stable.

Being Sunday the feed store was closed. She asked the hostler in the stable if Mrs. Bell was around.

" No, ma'am. Sundays Bessie generally stays home."

" Mr. Kump told me he kept a mare here that I could use," she said. " Do you have a side-saddle ? "

" Side-saddle ? " The hostler looked incredulous. " There's a relic up in the loft all covered with green velvet that might be one, but it ain't been used for years. Look : If you want to ride, why don't you go over an' borry a divided skirt from Bessie ? The only sensible way to ride is a-straddle, beggin' yore pardon, M'om."

" If you don't mind I'll use the side-saddle," Daphne said coldly. " I don't think I'll go far."

The hostler shrugged, and presently led out a neat little sorrel mare wearing what had once been an expensive side-saddle.

Daphne was used to horses, but her riding had been astride. She knew Bessie would gladly lend her a divided skirt, but she was too proud to ask favours while she was engaged in trying to send the man Bessie loved to prison.

The mare seemed gentle, and she mounted without any great difficulty. The mare struck out at an easy gallop, and for a while Daphne let her have her head.

It occurred to her then that the mare knew where she was going, and in all likelihood they would soon wind up at the K Bar K ranch, and the first person she probably would see was Hondo Horn—the last man she wanted to see. She slowed the mare down then, and headed into the nearby green hills.

The mare was easy-gaited, and Daphne found herself enjoying the ride, and delighted with the scenery as she went from one timbered canyon to another, getting many miles farther from town than she realized.

She came out on a ridge presently, and stopped beside a great, flat rock some forty feet square and dismounted. Leaving the sorrel mare stand she walked out on the rock and gazed down upon a great, semi-circular basin of almost breath-taking beauty. She didn't know it, but she was looking down into Swan Basin, and she could see no way of getting down there.

She sat for some time enjoying the sheer beauty and grandeur of the place while the mare grazed around with dragging reins. Aware that it must be long past noon she realized that she had better be getting back to town. She caught the mare, examined the girth, led the animal up beside the flat rock and mounted easily. She was determined not to go back the way she had come.

For some time she rode along the comb of the basin, but she found no trail into it. She was Westerner enough to keep track of her directions, and she knew that she was getting a little nearer town—unless she had to retrace her course. She was getting into a wilder country than she had bargained for, but as yet she wasn't in the least alarmed.

And then, suddenly she was. A cry, the most ghastly she had ever heard, beat upon her ears. It made her blood run cold.

For a minute she didn't know whether it was human or animal. Then it came again, and this time she knew that it was undeniably human.

Someone was in trouble. She was scared stiff, but the demands of common humanity were not to be denied. She knew in which direction the sounds had come from, and she urged the mare forward at a swift trot, her hooves making scarcely any sound over the thick, slippery pine grass.

She saw a clump of tall pines through the aspens, but now the hillside tipped so steeply that she had to draw the mare down to a walk. She forced her way through the aspens, and suddenly saw a small clearing surrounding the clump of pines. Nor was that all. What froze her whole body with horror and made her tongue cleave to the roof of her mouth was the sight of a man dangling from the limb of a tree with nothing beneath his feet but vacant space.

There were two men on horseback watching the man's frenzied struggles, and as she saw them the man again gave that fearful cry. Then she recognized the two hangmen. They were Hondo Horn, and his friend, Pat Young!

A cry of horror escaped her lips before she could stifle it. Instantly both men whirled to face her, and she had a blurred vision of Pat Young reaching for his gun.

She had come upon an abominable crime being committed, and she had no other idea than that she would be killed herself.

But she had to voice a protest if it cost her life the next instant.

"You cowards!" she cried out. "You contemptible cowards!"

The hanging man had swung around so that he could see her.

"Help! Help!" he bellowed.

As yet it hadn't occurred to her that if the man was being strangled by a rope that he couldn't yell for help.

"Company, Hondo," Pat said. "What d'ye know!"

Then only did Daphne see that the unfortunate victim was hanging by his arms, and by two ropes. Yet it was torture, and a rather ingenious form of the same. One rope was fastened around the man's wrist, and it went up over a huge tree limb and down to the horn of Pat Young's saddle, where it was dallied But the other rope was fastened only to a thumb. It went over the limb the same way, and was dallied to the horn of Hondo's saddle. Right now Hondo's rope was almost slack so that the fellow's weight was all upon his wrist. But if Pat should slack away and Hondo tighten his dallies the weight would all be upon the thumb, and excruciating agony would result.

"Fer Gawd's sake, miss, make 'em quit," the hanging man pleaded. "They're killin' me by inches."

"I told you we shoulda gagged him for a while," Pat remarked.

Daphne didn't know exactly what she could do, but she drove forward with the idea of getting her horse where the man could rest his weight on it. But Hondo was too quick for her. He slipped his rope from the saddle horn, passed it over to Pat, and caught her horse by the bit.

"Since you've butted in on the show we'll give you a grandstand seat, but you can't take the stage," he told her grimly.

The big dull looking fellow swinging underneath the limb was making the air vibrate with his piteous clamour. Daphne didn't know who he was, but she thought she had seen him in Highline.

Hondo swung down, and before she knew what he was up to he had lifted her from the saddle.

"You beast! You vile, murderous beast!" she screamed at him. Then she became paralyzed with terror as, holding her by one arm with ridiculous ease, he dragged her over to where a third horse stood, and began to take a lasso rope from the saddle. For a minute she thought he might be going to hang her, too.

He dropped the noose of the rope over her head and pinned her arms to her body. In desperation she made a futile grab at the handle of his sixgun.

"You caught you a regular wildcat," Pat Young said admiringly.

Hondo dragged her over to a smaller tree, and bound her to it so that she faced the hanging man.

"I hope you don't scream, because I'd hate to have to put a gag in your mouth," he told her unrelentingly.

She didn't answer. She saw now that the man had been stripped of his shirt, and she noticed a long black-whip coiled over a broken limb of the same tree. Across the thin undershirt she could see a single thin dirty smear.

"All right, Ozark, ready to talk now, or do we go on with the show?" Hondo asked.

The man had lapsed into sullen silence.

Hondo remounted his horse and took back his rope. "Slacken away," he ordered Pat, and suddenly the man's weight was transferred from his left wrist to his right thumb.

Daphne saw the man's eyes almost start from his head with the agony. He bit his lower lip for a second, and then a yell that dwarfed all his previous efforts burst from his throat.

Daphne fainted.

Chapter XII A Plain Case of Murder

It was not sadism which caused Hondo to force the girl to witness what was about to take place. He was nauseated himself by the task he had set himself to do, and he felt extreme pity for her. But now that she had blundered on to the scene he knew that his only chance for justification lay in compelling her to witness the results.

The night before he had set a guard over the granary at the ranch, but no one had showed up. That morning he and Pat Young had ridden away on a quiet hunt, after warning Ben Dambeau and others to carefully watch the place. But he didn't believe the Thornberrys had the nerve to invade the K Bar K in broad daylight.

His anger against his brutal enemies had been increased by the results of Dr. Beck's examination of Owen Denny. In addition to the frightful whipping he had received it was the doctor's opinion that one of the boy's kidneys had been kicked loose. The doctor had insisted upon taking Owen back to town with him, and there was a chance that he might have to operate.

" Who kicked you, Owen ? " Hondo asked.

" It was that damned Ozark," Owen replied. " He kicked me twice."

That Sunday morning Hondo and Pat rode away from the ranch together. It was almost noon when they saw the man they were looking for. Ozark, as usual, was fighting his horse, a half-broken bronco, when they saw him coming down a trail. It was brush country, and they turned aside quickly, one on each side of the trail. Pat had his rope on the fellow before Ozark knew that there was anyone within miles of him.

They had taken the ruffian back to the nearest large trees. He had cursed and threatened, but no word did he get out of them until he stood beneath the tree limb with the ropes on him. First, however, they had removed his coat and shirt.

Hondo told him quietly what they were going to do. To emphasize it he took down the black-whip they had brought along for that purpose, and gave the fellow one quick, stinging lash that ran around his body like fire. It brought the first yell from Ozark.

" You helped torture Owen Denny yesterday," Hondo said. " He says you were the worst one. Doc Beck says you kicked one of his kidneys loose. But that ain't what we're after you for."

" What're you goin' to do to me ? " the bully bleated then.

" We're going to hang you up by one thumb. If that one pulls out by the roots we'll put the rope on the other one. If we have to we'll take the last bit of hide off your back with this black-whip. That is unless you tell us something."

" Tell yuh what ? " Ozark growled.

" Who murdered Tim Bell ? " Hondo shot out.

Ozark's great heavy jaw sagged ; his sly, piggish little eyes betrayed surprise—and fear. He gulped twice, and only a suggestive writhing of the black-whip brought a stammering answer from him.

" H-how should I know? W-wasn't he killed accidental? "

" You know damn well he wasn't," Hondo charged. " He was murdered, and you know who done it. I think you were picked to do the job because you're the best rifle shot in the country."

"You're crazy," the man muttered, but he couldn't seem to get his slack jaws to stop clicking.

"I've been a long time figuring this thing out," Hondo remarked to Pat. "What fooled me was that we took it for granted Tim had been killed Tuesday because he had told Bessie he would be home that night. But he was actually murdered Wednesday morning And the reason he didn't come home was because he was in a poker game.

"I knew Tim would never stay all night with the Thornberrys even for a poker game but meeting them at a camp out on the range was a different matter Especially if there was somebody else along who didn't belong to their crowd."

Ozark's piggy little eyes contracted painfully as he listened intently to every word.

"What happened was," Hondo went on, "Tim met up with the Thornberrys at an old prospector's cabin at the head of Swan Basin. They got in a poker game, and as usual Tim took all their money. The nex. morning they laid for him and shot him with a rifle so it would look like somebody had mistaken him for a deer. Now you go on from there, Ozark."

"I don't know nothin', an' I won't tell nothin'," the fellow said stubbornly.

"Then I reckon we'll have to do some persuading, Pat," Hondo said, and there was genuine reluctance in his voice.

They had just begun to work on him when Daphne Dixon made her unfortunate appearance.

"Look," Pat exclaimed when the girl fainted. "What'll we do?"

"Go ahead," Hondo said grimly "She'll come to. If we have to kill this hombre we'd better do it while she's unconscious."

"Stop! I can't stand any more," Ozark yelled as his weight once more came upon his macerated thumb. "I'll talk."

They promptly shifted his weight back to his wrist.

"He was murdered," the fellow blubbered. "It was like you said, only——"

"Who shot him?" Hondo rasped out.

"The Dixon kid. He was——"

The report of a rifle cut short the sentence. Ozark's body seemed to leap in the air, and then he was a dead, inert weight upon Pat's rope.

Momentarily too stunned to do anything else the men slipped their dallies and allowed the body to fall to the ground. There was a smear of blood on the front of Ozark's undershirt, and a rapidly spreading larger one on the back. He had been centered by a bullet.

Hondo looked at Ozark, and then he looked at Daphne. The girl had come out of her faint, and was looking at the body of the dead man with frozen horror!

Then her gaze turned to Hondo with inexpressible loathing. "You—you murderer," she whispered.

Already Pat had gone in search of the man who had murdered Ozark, but in that brushy, timbered section there was little or no chance that he could be found.

Hondo went over and released Daphne from the tree. "We didn't kill him," he said dully.

"Why lie to me?" she cried out furiously. "I'm not blind. Now I suppose you'll murder me to cover up your crime."

It was the rifle shot that had brought Daphne out of her faint. She hadn't heard anything that Ozark said. But Hondo didn't know that. He thought she had heard the man accuse her brother of murder. To save him she would persistently contend that he and Pat had murdered Ozark.

"No," he said wearily, "we're not going to murder you. You're free to go any time you want, but you had better let us show you the way to a trail. You might get lost."

Her handbag had fallen on the ground while Hondo was tying her up and it had come open. A long, folded sheet of paper had fallen out of it. Hondo picked up the bag, and then the paper. It came unfolded in his hand, and his eyes suddenly fastened upon his own name.

The document he scanned was a deposition by Bill Burgess swearing that he had seen and overheard Hondo Horn giving Willard Dixon money with which to buy hay from Sep Kokler.

Daphne stood watching him read the deposition. "It won't do you any good to destroy it, because Mr. Burgess will make another one," she declared.

He knew what this meant. If Burgess swore to that story on the stand, or even this deposition was presented, young Dixon would be acquitted, and Hondo would promptly be arrested, unless the story was broken down.

"You can have it back," he said. "It must have cost you quite a lot of money."

Daphne flushed guiltily. She was frightened and shocked. She wanted to run, but didn't quite dare.

Methodically Hondo lifted the big body of Ozark and lashed it firmly across the man's own saddle. He had just finished when Pat returned.

" He got away," Pat said regretfully. " From the signs I take it he had been following sweetheart here."

" A good guess then it would be Rumel Thornberry, but we can't prove it," Hondo said.

" You're takin' Ozark ? "

" Nothing else to do."

Hondo held the sorrel mare while Daphne mounted, but he didn't offer to assist her, and she would have shrunk at the touch of his hand.

She followed along behind the two men as they travelled single-file down the steep slope. An hour and a half later they came upon a road several miles below where Swan Creek left its canyon.

" All you have to do now, Miss Dixon, is follow this road. It'll take you right into Highline," Hondo said.

She rode past them, and as soon as she was well ahead of them set the sorrel mare at a gallop.

" That was foolish," Pat said. " She'll tell her yarn, and we'll meet a reception committee with ropes."

" I want her to tell her story first," Hondo said. " Only, I hope it is to the sheriff, and not to Slick Abel."

" Where are we goin' ? " Pat asked.

" We're going to take this carrion home—where it belongs. If only one of 'em is missing we'll know he is the murderer."

They turned back the other way, and were soon in sight of the Thornberry ranch. Now that Ozark's mount was headed home they no longer led it. They turned into a short lane leading from the main road to the Thornberry buildings, and at the end of the lane they were seen.

Four men came off the shaded east porch of the squat log house. They were Ezra Thornberry, Brig Dow, Gus Marks—— and Slick Abel.

Hondo and Pat stopped in the yard, while Brig Dow went over and caught the horse carrying the dead man.

" There's your dog, Thornberry," Hondo said. " You can do as you please with it."

" What—what does this mean ? " Abel spluttered. "This looks like murder."

"Right you are, Slick, and you may have some fun getting Rumel off."

Their astonished looks showed him that they had beaten the murderer back to the ranch, and since Rumel was not there it seemed certain that he or Lafe Lufkin was the murderer—and the odds were on Rumel.

"What yoh givin' us? Rumel wouldn't kill Ozark," Ez contended.

"Not even to keep him from telling us all about the way Tim Bell was murdered?" Hondo laughed harshly, mirthlessly. "You can tell Rumel," he said, "that he was a bit too late. Ozark had already talked."

They swung about, but as they retreated they kept their eyes upon the men until they were halfway down the lane. Then they let their horses out to a lope.

"Well, where now?" Pat queried.

"To town."

"Not me," Pat said quietly. "I got to tell you something, Hondo. Something I feel like a dog for having to tell. I lied to you when I said I just wanted a place where I'd have a chance to go straight."

"How's that, Pat?"

"I led you to think I'd been pardoned. I wasn't. I broke out of the pen. Nobody was killed, but there was a guard or two got a cracked head. It'll be life for me if I'm caught, likely. I'm sorry I done you dirt."

"It's all right, Pat. I owe you plenty for coming back of your own free will when you found out I was serving time for what you done."

"If we hadn't been friends in the first place I never would have done it," Pat said. "And you drug me out of a river once, remember?"

"You'd better pull your freight, Pat."

"I aim to. And you'd better come with me."

"I'll stick it out."

"I hate to leave you," Pat said apologetically. "I can't see a chance to beat this rap, and that sheriff would soon have the goods on me anyway. But I sure would like to know how this comes out."

"Listen: Sep Kohler is still herding sheep, and his cabin has been empty ever since Willard Dixon was arrested there. There's bound to be some grub left. You hang out there a day or so and if I'm in jail I'll have the old man send Spike

Williams out with supplies. You can trust Spike," Hondo stated.

"You got a lot of confidence in Kump, too, ain't you?"

"He's a guy you can tie to," Hondo replied briefly.

They shook hands and parted. Then Hondo rode on alone toward Highline to face the accusation of murder which Daphne Dixon would have brought against him.

Chapter XIII "They're Holding Hondo for Murder"

Daphne was so ill from shock that she could scarcely keep her balance in the side-saddle, yet somehow she managed to keep the sorrel mare at a gallop until Highline loomed in view.

She had to ride past the livery stable, and although she had intended going straight to the courthouse she stopped when she saw Bessie Ball standing in front of the stable. She would be glad to get out of the saddle and go the rest of the way on foot.

"Good heavens, child, what happened?" Bessie cried. "You look as pale as a ghost. Don't tell me Fancy-foot threw you off."

"No, she was perfect," Daphne said, as she slid to the ground.

"Here, come into the office and sit down. I'll get you a drink of water—or a shot of whisky."

"No, I can't stop," Daphne refused. "I—I've got to see the sheriff."

"The sheriff! What happened?"

"Oh, I can't tell *you*," Daphne cried helplessly. "I—I saw something dreadful."

"Something to do with Hondo?" Bessie demanded.

"Yes, yes. He killed a man!"

"I know several he should have killed long ago," Bessie said unemotionally. "Who was it?"

"I don't know. They had whipped him, and then hung him up by his thumbs, and—and finally they—they murdered him."

Bessie stared at her a moment. "You're crazy," she said. "You've been out in the sun too long."

"It's true, I tell you," the girl cried. "That man Hondo tied me up and forced me to watch it."

"Now I know you're crazy," Bessie said, but Daphne was halfway across the street. Bessie ran and caught up with her.

"If that's the kind of a story you've cooked up in that addled brain of your's I'm going along to see the sheriff," she said.

They cut across behind the bank and reached the court-house without meeting anyone. Bessie prepounded a few questions, but Daphne refused to answer.

Sheriff Watson was just going out to supper, and his deputy was in the office.

"I warn you, Sheriff," Bessie said as they entered. "This girl is crazy as a cuckoo."

"I am perfectly sane," Daphne retorted. "I was tied up to a tree to-day and forced to witness the torture and then the murder of a helpless man."

"Well, this sounds interesting," Watson said. "Give the young lady your chair, Ace. Where did this happen, and who was the victim?"

Daphne bit her lip. Plainly the sheriff thought that she was out of her head, or concocting some monstrous lie, as Bessie did.

"I don't know who the victim was, but the murderers were Hondo Horn and Pat Young."

There were three chairs in the office. The sheriff occupied one of them, and the girls the other two. Ace Gillette leaned against the wall. The sheriff caught his deputy's eye meaningly.

"How come 'em to tie you up?" Watson asked.

"They were torturing the man when I accidentally rode up on them."

"Suppose now you just go ahead and tell us quietly how it all happened," the sheriff suggested.

Daphne calmed herself as best she could, told of her ride, and exactly what she saw when she encountered the three men.

"You mean to say he was hanging by his thumbs?" Watson asked.

"That's the way it looked to me. They had two ropes on him, and it seemed to me they were putting his weight first upon one arm and then the other."

"Then what happened?"

"Hondo gave his rope to the other man, and pulled me off

my horse, dragged me over to a tree and tied me there, facing the man."

"Did he say why?"

"He said I might as well see the rest of the show." At last her story was gaining credence. Even Bessie showed signs of conviction—and unhappiness.

"Before you go on tell us just what this victim looked like."

"He was a big man, light-haired, with small eyes."

"Did you notice his horse and saddle?" Gillette broke in.

"Yes. His horse was a bay with stocking legs. I remember it was covered with lather, and there was blood on its flanks where it had been spurred," Daphne remembered.

"Looks like the man might have been indulging in a little torture of his horse, too," the sheriff said.

"Ozark," Ace Gillette said succinctly.

The sheriff nodded. "Go on, Miss Dixon."

"After they tied me they drew the man up and he screamed so dreadfully I—well, I guess I fainted. Then I seemed to hear a shot, and when I looked up the man was falling."

"What happened after that?"

"Hondo released me. The other man went away, but he came back and said he couldn't catch whoever had fired the shot. He claimed somebody had been following me, but I don't believe there was any other man," Daphne asserted.

"Humph!" Bessie snorted. "We won't get the truth about this till Hondo gets in." She turned to Daphne. "If he had murdered that man like you say do you think he would have been fool enough to let you live to tell about it?"

"I thought he would kill me, but he didn't," Daphne acknowledged.

"Did he threaten you?" the sheriff asked quickly.

"No."

"Where is the body?"

"They brought it down to the road. I came on ahead. I suppose they are bringing it in."

"Sheriff, I think I'll get Doc Beck and start out," Gillette said.

"Yes, you'd better," the sheriff agreed. "Now, Miss Dixon, is there anything you *haven't* told us about this business?"

Daphne flushed. "Only one thing, I think," she said. "My handbag had fallen open, and a paper fell out of it. Hondo Horn picked the paper up and read it."

"What was in it?"

"It was the deposition of a witness for my brother in his coming trial. But he gave it back to me. "If you'd like to see it——"

The sheriff nodded and reached out his hand. Daphne handed over the deposition. His shaggy eyebrows lifted as he read the document.

"You're sure he read this?" he inquired.

"Yes."

"Well, I suppose it wouldn't have done him any good to tear it up. If this is true then it certainly clears your brother and convicts Hondo of stealin' them cattle," Watson said.

"And if he would steal cattle he would commit murder to cover it up," Daphne declared.

Bessie fairly snatched the paper from the sheriff's hand and scanned it hurriedly. "This is a damnable lie!" she cried, too angry to give way to tears.

"I don't think so," Daphne stated.

For a moment the two girls glared at each other. Daphne was the first to look away She knew she was right, yet, somehow, she felt ashamed.

"Did you examine the dead man closely, Miss Dixon?" the sheriff asked.

"No—o, I tried to keep my eyes off—it—as much as possible."

"Tell us what you did notice."

Daphne made an effort to recall Ozark's appearance. "I know he was wearing only an undershirt. There was a dark ring around it where he had been hit with a whip. I remember that there was blood on the front of his shirt, and when they tied him face downward across the saddle I know his whole back was a great smear of blood."

"You say you heard the shot and came out of your faint. Did you see a gun in either man's hand?" the sheriff persisted.

"No, I didn't," she said, "but what does it matter? They were brutally torturing the man whether they killed him or not."

"There was another torture case yesterday, my girl," the sheriff said sadly. "A nineteen-year-old boy was brutally whipped with bridle-chains, beaten and kicked, so that his health may be ruined all his life. But Hondo didn't do that. If the man you saw killed was who we thought it was he was one of the men who kicked Owen Denny, and used bridle-chains to whip him. But of course that doesn't mean that

Hondo was justified in taking the law into his own hands for revenge."

Daphne felt completely let down. She was physically tired from the ride, the harrowing things she had seen had wrecked her nerves, and now complete reaction had set in. Her head fell over on the sheriff's desk, and she gave way to long, body-racking sobs.

"Better let me handle her, Sheriff," Bessie said. "You go send up a rig from my stable."

Daphne's sobs were more restrained when Bessie's hostler, Hank, drove up to the courthouse door.

"Come now," Bessie said, "this is a public place and you can't be crying all over it. I've got a buggy outside, and I'm taking you to my place for the night."

"I don't want to go there," Daphne sobbed. "I know you hate me."

"Don't be silly," Bessie said. "Come along."

Daphne dried her eyes and walked out to where the rig waited. After a moment's hesitation she climbed in. She didn't intend to stay long with Bessie, but she dreaded the ordeal of going to the hotel before she had a chance to compose her swollen and tear-streaked face.

It was a pretty little house, tastefully furnished and kept. Bessie's living room was a pleasant place indeed after the barren front room of the ESMERALDA.

"You just relax on the couch here, and after a bit you can wash up," Bessie said. "I'll fix us some supper."

"Why should you be good to me?" Daphne asked. "You told me you were in love with Hondo Horn."

"I still am, and always will be. And you're his enemy, because you're being fooled. All right. I'm not afraid of you. If you wasn't his enemy then I might be scared. In that case you would have to look out."

Presently Daphne took a bath, and then she sat down at a tiny table to a meal that suited her taste better than any of which Nick Cropopolos had been so proud. After supper she made only mild protest when Bessie insisted that she sleep in the spare bedroom.

She was surprised when she awakened the next morning to find that she had slept soundly all night. The crisp odour of frying bacon and eggs seeped in from Bessie's kitchen.

She dressed hurriedly, washed her face and hands and entered the kitchen.

Bessie looked up soberly. "Feel better?" she asked.

"Yes, I feel fine. You've treated me awfully nice. You shouldn't have bothered to make breakfast for me."

"Think you'll be able to work in the bank today?" Bessie asked, ignoring the thanks.

"Yes, that is—if—if I still have a job."

"I think you will. George A. is funny. He's kinda big. Never holds petty grudges like the rest of us."

"Is—is there any news?" Daphne asked stiffly.

"Yes, I guess there is," Bessie answered tonelessly. "They're holding Hondo for murder."

"Oh."

"He didn't kill Ozark, but he gave himself up."

"I wish I could believe that."

"Eat your breakfast."

"Anyway," Daphne persisted, "they were torturing that man, whether they killed him or not. Even if somebody else had been tortured it was inhuman."

"Yes, I guess it was," Bessie sighed. "But it settled one thing."

"What was that?"

"Just before he was shot Ozark confessed that he knew who had murdered my husband," Bessie said. "You see, Hondo knew that the only way to ever prove anything was to force a confession from Ozark. But instead it didn't pan out. Now it looks like Hondo himself will be hanged.

The ominous words gave Daphne as much mental pain as a barbed wire suddenly striking could have hurt her body. She didn't want Hondo Horn to be hanged, despite his numerous crimes. And, now that she had had time to think it over she was not nearly so sure that somebody else might not have shot Ozark. She started to get her things.

"Come on back and drink some coffee," Bessie ordered kindly.

Daphne stopped. "You've every right to hate me," she said. "Why do you insist on treating me with kindness?"

"Frankly, you've got me there," Bessie said. "Maybe Hondo sized it up when he said, 'She wouldn't be much good if she didn't fight for her brother if she thinks he's innocent.'"

"Hondo Horn said that?"

"Last night. In fact, I think he's in love with you."

"Wh-what?" Daphne gasped. "That—that man—in love with me? Why it's ridiculous."

"Everybody is ridiculous in some way," Bessie philosophized. "Me more than anybody. I'm in love with Hondo, Hondo is in love with you, and you are trying to hang him. By rights I should have put poison in that coffee you're drinking, but I didn't. Maybe it's because I know Hondo never would marry me anyway. Maybe it's because I love him so much I can't help liking the people he likes."

Overwhelmed, Daphne burst into tears.

CHAPTER XIV — A BLOODY UNDERSHIRT

HONDO HORN heard Ace Gillette and Dr. Beck coming along the road and stopped. They were riding in a democrat wagon, with the deputy's saddle horse tied behind the rig. "Looking for me, Ace?" Hondo asked.

"Yes. Where's the body?" the deputy countered crisply.

"I left it at Thornberry's."

"Where's Pat Young?"

"He went after a clean shirt. Don't let me detain you. I'm on my way to see the sheriff."

"I wonder if I can bank on that?" Gillette wondered.

"Why not? Ever know me to lie?" Hondo challenged.

"No, but this is the first time you've been charged with murder. And there seems to be some new evidence in the Dixon case."

"I'm going in to surrender if the sheriff wants me," Hondo said evenly, "but I don't count on being taken in against my will."

"Okay, Hondo," Gillette said. "I believe you. But if you don't show up I'll be after you, and I won't be bluffing either."

They drove on, and Hondo continued toward town. Pat would be gone. It would be his story now against Daphne's. She would never say that Ozark had named her brother as Tim Bell's murderer, so there was no use for him to do it. Besides, he didn't believe that Willard had killed Tim. He still thought Ozark was the man, but that the fellow had been hired to do it by his employers. If he had had a few minutes more he would have found out the truth.

Although he had failed in his main objective a lot of things had been cleared up to his own satisfaction.

Ever since Tim Bell had been killed during deer hunting season the fall before he had had the feeling that it had been no accident. But his suspicions had been vague until Willard Dixon had given him the surprise of his life by alleging that Hondo had employed him to feed cattle at Sep Kohler's isolated ranch.

Hondo had liked Willard. He knew that the boy had one great weakness, a propensity to gamble. Unlike Tim Bell, who had a habit of winning, Willard nearly always lost.

Willard had been hunting the day Tim Bell was supposed to have been killed. He claimed that in the excitement of pursuing a wounded buck through the brush he had lost his horse, and darkness coming upon him had built a fire and spent the night in the hills. Since it was many miles from where Tim had been killed his story had been accepted.

Every hunter known to be anywhere in the country had been questioned as to their whereabouts. The Thornberrys and their two employees, Ozark, and Lafe Lufkin, had told a circumstantial story of having fixed fence all day, and spending the night at the ranch.

It had not occurred to Hondo to question either story until after Willard's arrest. He didn't believe the boy would have stolen the cattle except under some sort of compulsion. And he knew that Willard must have got the money he had paid Kohler from someone else.

His suspicions had fallen at once upon Brig Dow and the Thornberrys, but he had run into a blank wall until he had overheard a casual, wouldbe jocular remark upon the part of old Gus Marks about the condition of the Thornberry fences.

He had taken the trouble then to examine the fence which they claimed to have been fixing the day Tim was supposed to have been killed. There was no evidence of any work having been done at all.

Things had begun to dovetail. The Thornberrys had lied about being at home Tuesday. Tim Bell had promised his wife that he would be home Tuesday night, but he had not come. Willard Dixon had somewhat suspiciously lost his horse and been compelled to spend a night in the open. All of them were inveterate poker players.

Only then did it begin to dawn upon Hondo that Tim Bell might have been killed on Wednesday instead of Tuesday. His body had not been discovered until a search was made Thursday.

Soon after the snow was off Hondo had made a search of the vicinity where Tim had been killed, and some two miles from the spot he had come upon an old prospector's cabin. There was every indication that someone had camped there the preceding fall. There was still some wood that showed it had been cut about that length of time, and signs that there had been a fire of considerable duration in the still intact crude stone fireplace. And there were a number of empty tin cans and whisky bottles lying about.

Hondo had said nothing to anybody, but from that time on he was sure in his own mind that Tim Bell had met up with the Thornberrys and Willard Dixon, and yielding to his love for the poker game he had camped with them that night, probably winning all of their money and possibly considerable I O Us.

In the morning he had been stalked, and killed by one of them. Ozark, he guessed, because of the man's well-known expert marksmanship and his natural brutality. The money Tim had won had been taken from him, and somehow Willard Dixon had been convinced that he would be accused of the crime if it ever became known. From that time on the boy had become their tool.

The brutal beating of Owen Denny had given Hondo his clue as to how to extort a confession, and Pat Young had been a willing helper. And then, on the very verge of success, the one man who could be forced to tell the truth had been killed.

Hondo had no regrets for the methods he had employed. It had been a distasteful job, far more so after the unexpected appearance of Daphne Dixon, but he had gone ahead grimly as he would with any other disagreeable job such as marking and branding a calf.

He talked with the sheriff, and learned that Daphne had been at the courthouse with Bessie.

" I'd arrest you for murder, Hondo, except for one thing," Sheriff Watson told him. " That girl says she didn't see either of you have a gun in your hand. But I'll have to hold you till Ace and Doc gets back with the body."

" All right, Sheriff, you're the doctor."

" Evidently you must have got your education among the Apaches," the sheriff drawled. " What did you get out of him ? "

" An admission that Tim Bell was murdered last fall."

" Hunh ? Who done that ? " Watson blurted.

"I was just about to find out when a bullet cut short the conversation."

"You must have had some reason to suspect him."

"I had. Just suppositions which I couldn't very well prove, and a lie or two."

"Such as?"

"Such as the Thornberrys lying about being home on a certain Tuesday last fall. You remember they claimed to be fixing fence all day, all four of 'em. You ride out there you'll find their fence hasn't been repaired for years."

"Then you think Tim Bell was murdered by the Thornberrys?"

"It might have been one of them, or somebody they paid to do it. But Tim was killed the day after we thought he was."

"Well, in a way, it's too bad you got interrupted," the sheriff stated. "But you're lucky not to be hanged for it. By the way, where's Bill Older?"

"Who?"

"Alias Pat Young—*vice versa*."

"Been messing around, have you, Sheriff?"

"That's my job, Hondo. When you were sent up for robbin' that bank the man who voluntarily came back and confessed that he was the fellow who held the horses outside the bank called himself Bill Older. But he was an old friend of yours named Pat Young. When he broke out of the pen a while back he came to you for protection, and you gave it to him. Aiding a criminal to escape the law is a crime, Hondo."

"I didn't know Pat had broke jail. I thought he had been pardoned," Hondo said slowly. "But it wouldn't have made any difference. I'd have helped him anyway."

"That's the wrong attitude, Hondo"

"Maybe. Pat was wrong, but he was a hot-headed kid, and the men who robbed that bank had got him stirred up by telling him how the man who owned the bank had pulled a lot of dirty tricks—which he had."

"That didn't make Pat or the others a judge or jury," the sheriff pointed out. "I've got to know where he is."

"He's gone south."

The eyes of the two men met and clinched. "I don't believe it," Sheriff Watson said flatly.

Hondo was still in the sheriff's office when Gillette and Beck returned.

"Git the body?" the sheriff asked.

" Yes. It's on a slab at the undertaker's," Ace Gillette said. " I brought over his undershirt."

Ace spread the shirt out on the sheriff's desk. The back of it showed extensive powder burns!

The eyes of all three men dwelt upon Hondo as he examined the shirt. He betrayed no emotion of surprise, nor did he so much as bend over to examine it closely.

" If Ozark had been shot from a distance the way you said he was, Hondo," the sheriff pointed out slowly, " there wouldn't have been any powder marks on that undershirt."

Hondo didn't answer.

" What was your findin's, Doc ? " the sheriff asked.

" He died almost instantly. The bullet went clear through his carcass, so of course we've no way of knowing whether it came from Hondo's gun or not."

" Could a slug from a forty-five such as Hondo carries have went clear through a man ? "

" Fired from that distance it could easily."

" Well, Hondo, which one of you fired the shot, you or Pat ? " the sheriff asked.

" I told you where the bullet came from," Hondo answered tersely. His mind was in a riot. His instinct told him to get away while he could. Despite Ace Gillette's watchfulness he knew that he could get away by shooting one or two of them. But all three men had been his friends. They were square shooters. The sheriff was only doing his obvious duty.

" You want my gun, I take it, Sheriff," he said.

" I'll take it," the alert deputy said. " You just keep your hands where they are, Hondo."

Hondo smiled, and raised his hands level with his elbows while Ace secured his gun.

" Guess we'll have to fix you up a cell, Hondo. Better not put him too close to Willard Dixon, Ace," the sheriff directed.

Hondo went quietly to his cell. The sheriff had wanted to believe in his innocence, and so, perhaps, had the deputy. But in view of that bloody, powder blackened undershirt they couldn't doubt.

Those marks had not been there when Ozark had been killed. Daphne could testify to that fact if she wanted to. But she couldn't be expected to remove a rope from around Hondo's neck and put it around the neck of her brother.

Chapter XV — The Brutal Truth

It was time for Daphne to go to the bank before she got away from Bessie's house. She wasn't aware that Bessie had kept her there deliberately so that she couldn't go to Slick Abel's law office.

After what had happened she was far from sure that she wouldn't be told that her services at the bank were no longer needed.

Barker was alone in the bank. He greeted her frostily.

"You'd better make out notices for all notes that are past due, Miss Dixon," he said. "Mr. Kump stayed at the ranch last night. He hasn't got back yet."

The bank hadn't been opened five minutes when Attorney Abel appeared.

"Miss Dixon," he said urgently. "I've got to have a talk with you."

"I'll be very busy until Mr. Kump arrives," she said. "We're expecting him any time. Couldn't I come to your office then?"

"I'm sorry, but this is more important than your job here," Slick insisted. "I must see you at once. In my office."

"I guess you'll have to get along without me for a while, Mr. Barker," Daphne said apologetically.

Barker grunted. Whether he could or he couldn't, or whether he meant that it would suit him well enough to dispense with her permanently she couldn't tell.

"I suppose," she said, when she and the lawyer were on the street, "that it has to do with the Ozark murder."

"Yes—but we won't discuss it until we reach my office."

She glanced at him out of the corner of her eye. Somehow he looked more worried than triumphant

He locked the outer door of his office, and led her into the inner room. "Don't want to take chances on any eavesdropper to-day," he said grimly. "Sit down."

Daphne sat gingerly upon the edge of her chair. She had the feeling that she approached some sort of climax in her life.

She seemed fascinated by the shiny smoothness of the lawyer's bald head. Was that why they called him "Slick," she wondered.

"Fate must be working on our side for you to have witnessed that murder yesterday," he commenced "Quite a shock to see the life let out of a husky man right before your eyes, wasn't it?" He asked the question almost eagerly, and he seemed to lick his lips with a certain gusto. Daphne gathered somehow that it was a scene which the lawyer would have liked to witness. For the first time she began to be physically afraid of the man.

"I didn't actually see the man killed," she replied as quietly as she could. "It was shock enough to come out of a faint and see him dying."

"You mean you were in a faint when the shot was fired?"

"Yes. I had fainted, but I don't know how long I was unconscious. I have the impression that it was the sound of the shot that roused me."

"You didn't hear Ozark say anything then?" he asked eagerly.

"No—only to beg for mercy."

"Did it appear to you that he had refused to give them the information they wanted?"

"Yes. But Hondo Horn says the man confessed that he knew who had murdered Bessie Bell's husband."

"We are not concerned with what Hondo Horn says. He lied. Did he say who it was?"

"No."

Abel leaned back in his chair and lighted a cigar. His relief over something was evident.

Daphne waited.

"There was a six-shooter in Horn's hand, of course, when you revived," he shot out.

"No, there wasn't."

"What? How can you say that if it was the shot that revived you? He couldn't have had time to restore it to the holster."

"He didn't have a gun in his hand. Neither did the other man. I am sure of that now, for each one had hold of the reins with one hand, and a rope with the other," she said positively. "In fact, I'm sure now that someone else fired that shot."

Abel bounced to his feet. "Have you told anyone else that you thought that?" he demanded with sudden fury.

"No, I—I—may have told Mrs. Bell. I don't remember."

"Humph!" His voice reeked with disgust, and he smoked furiously.

"I'm not going to swear away the life of a man who may be innocent," she said, beginning to grow angry.

"I'm sorry I lost my temper." Abel shifted tactics suddenly. "I wouldn't wound you for anything. I may say that in our brief acquaintance you have grown very dear to me." He smirked.

Daphne was liking the interview less and less. His tone implied that he was actually making love to her.

"You wouldn't be able to say positively that you heard a shot at all, now would you?" he wheedled suddenly. "For all you know the shot might have been fired several seconds before you opened your eyes, don't you think?"

"That may be," she had to admit. "But the man was still suspended."

"But he might have hung there for seconds," Abel persisted. "A fast gunman like Hondo Horn could have reholstered his gun in half a second. Tell me, what were your first words when you revived?"

"I'm not exactly sure. I think I called Hondo a murderer."

"Ah! I want the exact words."

"Well, as nearly as I can remember," she said tiredly, "I said, 'You murderer!' Just that."

"And he said?——"

"'We didn't kill him.'"

"And you said?——"

"I asked him what was the use of lying to me," she answered, trying hard to recall exact words. "I said, 'I'm not blind. Now I suppose you'll murder me to cover up your crime.' But——"

"Never mind the 'buts,'" he interrupted. "The fact remains that at the time you were convinced in your mind that Hondo Horn had shot Ozark while the man was helplessly suspended in the air."

Daphne said nothing.

"That is true, isn't it?" he demanded.

"Yes, but——"

"That is what you will testify on the witness stand. Now we come to an even more important point. The powder burns on Ozark's undershirt. You noticed those, of course."

"No, I did not!" she denied vehemently.

"But they were there, and you got a good look at the back of his shirt—or didn't you?"

"Yes, I did. I got sick every time I looked at it when they were bringing him out face downward across the saddle."

"Good. And the undershirt showed very pronounced burns, didn't it?"

"I know it did not. I noticed that except for the blood it looked very clean, although it had been torn at the shoulder. The only smudge on it was where they seemed to have struck him with a whip. But I noticed that while the man was still alive."

Abel glared at her through clouds of cigar smoke until she began to fidget uneasily.

"How do you account for the fact, then, that the undershirt which the officers took off the dead man shows very pronounced powder burns—as if a gun had been fired at it from a distance of not more than three feet?" he demanded belligerently.

"I don't know," she replied in a quavering voice. "I only know there were no powder marks on it when the body was loaded on to the horse."

"But that," Abel said gently, "is not what you're going to testify."

"I don't know what you mean."

"I mean that you are going to testify that almost the first thing you noticed after you revived from your faint was that circular black splotch," he all but hissed.

"Do you think that I would go on the witness stand and swear to a lie?" she demanded hotly.

"Why not? You paid Bill Burgess a thousand dollars to do it."

Daphne had half risen. She sank back in her chair with every bit of colour drained from her face.

"I paid him a thousand dollars to tell the truth," she cried defensively, but already she knew that it wasn't true.

"I'm your lawyer," Abel said with an air of long-suffering tolerance. "Why pretend anything with me? You know, and I know, and your brother knows that Bill Burgess never saw Hondo give Willard any money."

"You'll be saying next, I suppose, that Hondo didn't give him any money at all," Daphne said weakly.

"Of course he didn't. You weren't fooled about that, too, were you?"

Daphne's head was going round and round. The thick cigar smoke nauseated her, helped create the impression of total unreality. She told herself this was some kind of a horrid nightmare. But it was real. There was nothing illusory about that cynically smiling man with the bald head seated on the other side of the desk.

"You mean that Willard is a thief after all?" she forced herself to ask.

"I didn't say that," Abel smiled. "Hondo didn't give him any money He was up there feeding cattle which he knew were stolen, so the assumption must be that he intended to profit from the sale of them."

"Oh, I'm sick of it all, and I'm sick of you," Daphne cried out in utter disgust. "If Willard is guilty he'll have to plead guilty. I'll have no part in destroying the character of an innocent man."

His hard eyes seemed to hold her to her chair.

"You mean Horn? You saw an example of his character yesterday, didn't you?"

"If you are trying to frame him for stealing you would try to frame him for murder, too," she charged.

"Perhaps," he smiled. "Hondo is a dangerous man. The country would suit me a great deal better, and he vastly more profitable to me and my friends if Hondo were eliminated. Therefore"—he shrugged—"I eliminate him."

"Not with my help you won't," Daphne said fiercely, at last forcing herself to her feet.

"What about your brother?" Abel asked mildly.

"He said he *wanted* to be convicted. He'll have to get his wish."

"But he was talking about conviction for the theft of the cattle," he pointed out as she reached the door. "Not about being convicted of murder."

Daphne stopped as suddenly as if he had dropped a rope around her shoulders "What—did—you—say?" she got out.

"I was talking about murder, my dear. I didn't want to have to ever spring this upon you, but your own refusal to co-operate makes it necessary."

"I don't believe Willard is a murderer," she said weakly. "Who do you claim he ever killed?"

"Now I think you're beginning to act sensibly," the lawyer said. "Come on back and sit down." When she complied he resumed. "The man Willard murdered was named Tim Bell. He was Bessie's husband. He was a lucky gambler. Your brother liked to gamble. Tim Bell won all Willard's wages in a poker game. Because he suspected that Bell was crooked Willard shot Bell where it would appear someone had done it accidentally.

"Unfortunately for Willard there were no less than four witnesses to the crime. To make sure that they could prove it if they wanted to they relieved Willard of an I O U note for five hundred dollars made out on a Bell Feed & Livery Company letterhead and signed by your brother which he hadn't had a chance to destroy. The note is still in existence, and three of the four witnesses are still alive."

With perhaps the greatest effort of her life Daphne forced herself to be calm.

"The witness who is dead, I presume, is the man called Ozark," she said.

"You're catching on fast, my dear. Those men wanted to get rid of Hondo Horn. For one thing Hondo was the only one who suspected that Bell had been murdered, and eventually he would have uncovered the truth. So it was to Willard's interest, aside from the fact that he had no choice, to feed those stolen cattle, and then accuse Hondo of paying him to do it.

"Thanks to the testimony of Bill Burgess Willard will be acquitted. When that happens there will be nothing for the sheriff to do except arrest Hondo for the theft—unless he is convicted of murder before then. That is what we intend to fight for."

"To convict Hondo of killing Ozark when you know that he didn't do it?" she said in horror.

"I propose to convict him," he said grimly.

"And that means that—that I——"

"It means that you listen quietly while Bill Burgess gives his testimony in your brother's case, and when Hondo is arraigned for murder you will go on the stand and testify that when you saw Ozark's undershirt immediately after the murder it was exactly in the same condition in which it will appear in the courtroom," Abel said harshly.

"I will not do it," Daphne cried out her refusal. "What do you think I am, a murderess?"

"You'll be responsible for the hanging of your own brother if you refuse," Abel told her grimly. "And you will go to the penitentiary yourself for subornation of perjury. I hate to remind you, but I happen to hold your note for five hundred dollars, which is proof that you used a considerable sum of money as soon as you got here. In addition I took the precaution of getting a signed statement from Bill Burgess confessing that he agreed to commit perjury for the sum of one thousand dollars advanced by you."

"And what if I tell the truth about the whole thing?" Daphne demanded wildly.

"My dear girl, must you insult my intelligence? I have documentary proof to support my case. Your word would be totally unsupported. And think of the motive! The saving of your brother's life."

Once Daphne had seen a terrified little kitten cornered by a savage dog. She knew now exactly how that kitten had felt.

Chapter XVI — A Surprised Deputy

Hondo's cell was at the end of the corridor next the outside door. Anyone going to see Willard Dixon would have to pass directly in front of Hondo to get there. But Hondo had visitors before Willard did.

The first to call upon him were George A. Kump and Bessie Bell. He was not surprised to see them.

"Look here," George A. said, what kind of monkey business is this? Ain't I got troubles enough without you getting yourself in jail?"

"Didn't you ever try an experiment that backfired?" Hondo retorted.

"Plenty of times. But I never got locked up for it."

"If you two try to get funny about this I'll scream," Bessie warned them.

Sheriff Watson opened the cell door, and told them to enter, but he left the door open and waddled away.

"Well, I guess the first thing is to get a lawyer for you,"

Kump said. " There's none here. I talked to Judge Tillman. He says he'll hold off the preliminary hearing till we can get one, unless you want to waive it altogether."

" In that case I have to lay here for months till the trial comes up," Hondo said.

" I'm afraid you'll have to anyway."

" Unless I leave now."

Both visitors glanced toward the unlocked cell door. They knew what he was thinking. Hondo could probably overpower Sheriff Watson with his bare hands. They broke into protest in unison.

" Forget it," Hondo smiled. " I'll stay. I've got a brother that's a lawyer. I suppose he would be glad to come, but I hate to bother him. No, I think I'll just take a chance on representing myself at the preliminary hearing. Tell Judge Tillman to let 'er buck—any time he's a mind to."

" It looks bad," Kump warned. " That business of the powder burns is the worst."

" Has Daphne—Miss Dixon, I mean—said anything to either of you ? " Hondo asked anxiously.

" No. She came to work in the bank this morning, but Slick Abel took her up to his office before I got to town. She got back after a while when I was there, and said she wouldn't be able to work for me any more."

" You shouldn't have hired her in the first place," Bessie said.

" I told her to take the rest of the day off, and maybe she would change her mind," George A. said, ignoring Bessie.

" Before I forget it," Hondo said to them, " I want you to send Spike Williams up to Sep Kohler's place with some supplies. He'll find Pat Young there. Have him tell Pat the sheriff is looking for him, and for him to hustle out of here."

" You think that's the right thing, Hondo ? " George A. asked.

" Pat is all right. He's always had a lot of tough breaks."

" All right. I'll see that Spike warns him," George A. promised. " Now I think I'll leave you two alone a few minutes. I want to talk to young Dixon while I've got a chance."

He strolled down the corridor to where Willard stood clasping the bars of his cell.

" Hello, Willard," the banker greeted in a friendly tone. " How are you getting along ? "

Willard ignored the inquiry. " What have they got Hondo in here for ? " he demanded. " I hollered at him, and asked, but all he would say was ' murder.' I asked the deputy and he just said the same thing I'm goin' crazy Who did he kill ? "

" Ozark—they claim. Hasn't your sister told you ? "

" I haven't seen her since Hondo came."

" Willard, you know Hondo didn't give you any money. Ain't it about time you told the truth ? If you pleaded guilty it wouldn't go hard on you," Kump said.

" If he's going to hang it won't hurt him to be accused of cattle rustling," the boy snarled.

" Your sister is a fine girl. Good hand in the bank, too."

Willard went over to his bunk and buried his face in his hands. Kump's efforts to get anything out of him were futile, and the banker returned to Hondo's cell.

As soon as Kump started off to see Willard Bessie put her arms around Hondo's neck. " Kiss me, Hondo," she ordered.

He looked down at her with amused eyes. " Not going sentimental on me, are you, Bessie ? " he asked.

" No," she said while the word seemed to stick in her throat. " I just want you to feel that I'm for you, no matter what you do."

" I know that, Bessie," he said, and kissed her.

" You've got to fight this case, Hondo," she said with sudden anger. " You're taking it lying down. You've got to have a lawyer, and a good one. One who'll be smarter than Slick Abel. I don't know your brother. He may be good, but I want somebody else, too."

" Why ? " he asked. " If Daphne swears that I murdered Ozark I'll hang no matter who the lawyer is."

" Not if we can break down her story. If we can send her brother to the pen a smart lawyer might prove she was acting through malice."

" Her brother won't go to the pen."

" What ? "

" A paper fell out of her purse up there. I saw it. It was a deposition from Bill Burgess swearing he saw me pass Willard the money."

"I saw it, too," Bessie said angrily. "That dirty, whisky-soaked old bum. Nobody will believe him."

"He'll clear Willard and convict me."

"They bought him."

"Naturally."

Just then Kump returned. "Can't do a thing with him," he sighed.

The sheriff returned and they went away.

An hour or so later Daphne came to visit her brother. Ace Gillette let her into the corridor. She stopped for just a moment in front of Hondo's cell. Her hand went uncertainly to her breast, then she followed Ace down to her brother's cell.

Ace stopped for a moment at Hondo's cell on his way back. "Sorry about all this, Hondo," he said. "It's my job to gather evidence to convict you, but if there is anything that might be favourable let me know. I've just come back from where Ozark was killed, and what I found there won't help you any."

"You didn't see any sign of Rumel Thornberry being in the vicinity?"

"I'm sorry to say I didn't."

"Well, thanks, anyway, Ace."

"By the way Judge Tillman told me to tell you the preliminary hearing would come off at ten in the morning unless you asked for more time."

"It's all right with me."

Daphne was with her brother twenty minutes. Then Gillette came to take her away. She was weeping and kept her face covered with a handkerchief while she hurried past.

Hondo had little idea of the drama of that whispered conference between brother and sister.

This was the first interview in which Daphne had failed to greet her brother with a kiss.

"You're a long time getting here," Willard complained bitterly. "I can't find out anything. What about Ozark? When did Hondo kill him, and how?"

There was nobody in the adjoining cell, nor across the corridor, yet Daphne spoke in an almost inaudible whisper. "He didn't kill him."

"What? But Kump and the sheriff said——"

"I was there. I happened to faint, so I didn't see him actually die, but I know Hondo didn't kill him. But I've got to testify that he did."

"What? You know Hondo didn't kill him, yet you're going to swear he did."

"You know he didn't give you any money, too, yet you're going to swear he did, aren't you," she asked.

"But—but that is different," he mumbled.

"It's exactly the same, and for the same reason, Willard. It's so you won't be hanged for killing Tim Bell."

"But I didn't kill Bell," he blurted.

"You don't need to hold anything back any more, Willard. You see, when I refused to lie Hondo on to the gallows Slick Abel told me everything."

"That dirty, sneakin' coyote," Willard breathed viciously. "The next time I git him in this cell I'll choke the gizzard out of him with my bare hands. Did he tell you I killed Tim Bell?"

"Yes, he told me everything. Even to what a fool I was to pay Bill Burgess to commit perjury. Now they can even send me to the penitentiary if they want to."

"Daphne, I told you Bill Burgess didn't see me take any money," he cried.

"I know you did, but you acted so strangely I didn't know what to think. He made me believe he did."

"Tell me just what Abel told you," Willard said more composedly than he had yet spoken.

Still speaking in a whisper Daphne told him.

"And you're going to swear to that lie?" he asked.

"I don't know. I don't know what to do," she moaned. "Oh, Willard, I'm afraid I can't go through with it. I don't know why, but I—I feel some way about Hondo Horn that frightens me. I hated him when I thought he was trying to frame you, and—and yet he attracted me. Now——"

"Now you're in love with him!" Willard interrupted. "Caesar's Cats! Well, anyway we know what to do."

"We do? I've never been more confused in my life," she whimpered. "I'd go to jail in a minute rather than lie about giving Burgess that money, but—oh, Willard, why did you have to kill that man?"

"I—Oh, let it go. I'll plead guilty. You just tell the truth. It's the only way out now."

Daphne couldn't speak for tears, but she nodded vigorously. They clung to each other in utter desolation for a minute or so, and when the deputy came down the corridor she kissed Willard, and stood waiting to be let out.

Hondo could not be blamed for not guessing what kind of an interview it had been.

Hondo paced his cell like a caged tiger. It wouldn't be long now until Pat Young would be on his way to some even more remote fastness to escape the long arm of the law. Hondo wished desperately that he could be with him. He made up his mind to ask Bessie to smuggle in a gun. She would do it if he asked her. But when he pictured himself outside with a gun he knew that he wouldn't join Pat. Not, at least, until several chores were attended to.

He ate his supper, and because there was nothing else to do flung himself upon his bunk. There was only a single ceiling lamp burning on the second floor of the courthouse. The corridor between the cell rows was gloomy . neither dark nor light.

Suddenly he heard someone unlocking the door to the cell block, and curiosity caused him to swing his feet on to the floor.

It proved to be Ace Gillette. "This is crazy business, Hondo," the deputy stopped to say, "and I think it's a mistake."

"You think what's a mistake?" Hondo asked.

"What George A. has just done. He's put up ten thousand dollars bail money to get young Dixon out of here, and I know damn' well he's waitin' downstairs to give him more money to skip his bond. The old man must think a hell of a lot of you to waste money like that."

"But why——"

Gillette had gone on, but Hondo didn't need to ask the question. He knew why. The old man believed in his innocence, and he figured that if he could get Willard Dixon out of the country his sister might refuse to testify against Hondo.

Unfortunately, Hondo thought, there were some things that the old man didn't know.

Gillette and Willard came walking back up the gloomy corridor. It appeared almost as though Willard was reluctant to leave. Hondo saw the boy's face just before Ace started to unlock the door, and it startled him.

Suddenly Hondo saw Willard reach out as furtively, but as swiftly and surely as a cat's paw and lift the sixgun from the deputy's holster just as the door into the cell block swung open.

"Hey, what the——" the deputy gasped out.

"Hold it, Ace," Willard grated. There was nothing boyish about him now. "Don't let out any yells. Back up here an' unlock Hondo's cell."

"Why, you're crazy," the deputy protested.

"You do as I say or I'll let daylight through you," Willard hissed.

The helpless and alarmed deputy had no choice but to obey. The cell door swung open.

"Git your hat, Hondo, and come on," Willard ordered. "We'll lock the deputy in there in your place."

Hondo hesitated. He didn't know what crazy scheme was in the boy's mind. For all he knew Willard might even be intending to kill him. But he had wanted out of there, and this was his opportunity. He picked up his hat, the only bit of personal property he had in the cell, and stepped outside. A moment later the deputy sheriff was locked on the inside.

"I warn you this is the worst possible thing either of you could do," Gillette told them. "Let me out of here and give me my gun and I'll promise to say nothing about the whole thing."

"Sorry, Ace, but I've got a few things outside I'd like to do," Hondo said.

The deputy collapsed upon the bunk and took his bewildered head in his hands. Why Kump should have put up bail in the first place for a prisoner who was accused of trying to rob him was a puzzle, but not nearly so much as why that prisoner should take advantage of his sudden and unexpected liberty to hold up an officer and liberate the man who was supposed to be his worst enemy.

Chapter XVII — Kohler's Ranch

Daphne was half consciously aware of excitement downstairs and in the street for some time before there came a knock on her door. She had even gone to the window of her still unlighted room and looked out on the dimly lighted streets of Highline. She had seen little knots of men forming and reforming as the men talked a little and scurried on to other groups.

At any other time she would have been more curious, but to-night she was entirely absorbed in her own troubles, and desolate with loneliness besides. To lie a man on to the gallows was simply unthinkable, but the knowledge that refusal would cost her own brother's life was a tragic horn in her dilemma. Her only consolation was a ragged bit of pride that Willard had determined of his own free will to plead guilty.

The knock came twice before she really heard it. "Come in," she called hesitantly, then remembered that she had locked the door.

She faced Bessie Bell.

"Good heavens, haven't you heard the news?" Bessie asked.

Daphne turned cold all over. "No," she said faintly. "What news? Wo—won't you come in?"

Bessie stepped inside and planted her back against the door. "Hondo has escaped," she announced dramatically.

Daphne's heart turned over. She couldn't have analyzed her feelings if her life had depended upon it, but her first impression was one of relief—and gladness. Then the implications assailed her. A man held for murder might have done any desperate thing.

"Was—was anybody hurt?" she queried.

"Not yet," Bessie said grimly, "but anything can happen. Hondo and your brother left together."

"But what does it mean?" Daphne cried.

"None of us know. George A., the benevolent old fool, put up a lot of money for your brother's bond. His idea was to get him out of the country so he couldn't testify against Hondo. You, too, I suppose. But Willard crossed up everybody, including Hondo it's my guess, by grabbing the deputy's gun and holding him up. He forced Ace to open Hondo's cell. They locked Ace in the cell and that's all anybody knows," Bessie informed her.

"When did all this happen?" Daphne asked finally.

"About an hour ago. The only person in the sheriff's office was George A. He was waiting to see Willard. They tied him up, and took the two horses he had brought, one for himself and one for Willard, and that's the last that's been seen of them. But it wasn't more than half an hour till the night jailer showed up and let Ace Gillette out of the cell. A posse has just gone after them."

"But what does it all mean?" Daphne repeated helplessly.

"That's what I come to ask," Bessie said. "I thought your brother might have told you something."

"He did. He told me he was going to plead guilty."

Bessie went over to the bed. She looked at the girl with wide, staring eyes. "Maybe we can begin to make sense out of it anyway," she said. "Willard had decided to plead guilty?"

"Yes, even though he knew it meant he would be accused of murder. Of the murder of your husband." Daphne's voice suddenly rang with pride. "And I was going to tell the exact truth, although that means I'll go to prison for—for subornation of perjury."

"Subor—what? You mean you kids decided to do the right thing this afternoon, no matter what the consequences?" Bessie gasped.

"I guess that's about it," Daphne replied. "You see I didn't know the truth until this morning. Until then I was sure that Willard was innocent, and that Hondo Horn was trying to frame him."

"Bessie's somewhat stubby arms went suddenly around the girl. "Why, bless your honest heart!" she cried, "I think that's the bravest thing I ever heard of. I couldn't have done it if I'd been in your shoes."

"It—it wasn't easy," Daphne said, fighting back her tears. "This means Willard will be accused of murder. He'll probably be killed before he'll surrender."

"Look at me," Bessie ordered. "Did Willard kill my husband?"

"I don't know," Daphne said. "I only know he said he would be hanged for that murder if he didn't do as Slick Abel, Brig Dow and the Thornberrys told him to."

" I just can't believe that he did," Bessie said slowly, " any more than I can believe that Hondo killed Ozark. But I wouldn't want to be the man who stood in Hondo's way now."

" I don't know," Daphne murmured. " Slick Abel told me that Willard killed Mr. Bell, and he says he has the evidence."

There was a sudden, violent knock on the door, and it opened before either girl could speak. Attorney Abel slid inside. There was moisture on his bald head, and his thin lips were cruel as a snarling cat's.

" I must ask you to leave this room at once, Mrs. Bell," he said curtly. " I have to talk to my client's sister."

" I ain't a bit sure I'm pulling out, Slick," Bessie returned slowly. " Your client's sister has just confessed to me that her brother murdered my husband, so I'm sort of interested."

Abel turned upon Daphne in a fury. " You mean to say you told her an idiotic thing like that ? " he stormed.

" You yourself told me he did. Willard didn't say so." Daphne retorted. " He only said he would be hanged for it."

" Don't you realize what this will mean to you ? " the lawyer demanded. " Death, a miserable coward's death on the scaffold for your brother—a long term in prison for you."

Despite her resolution Daphne paled and quivered.

" It may not be as bad as you think, Slick," Bessie said evenly. " It might even turn out to be you who will wind up behind bars—or on the gallows."

" On the contrary," the lawyer said crisply. " We can convict Hondo Horn for murder without this young lady's testimony. We can discredit her on the ground that George A. Kump paid ten thousand dollars to get her brother released, and since we can prove her guilty of subornation of perjury it won't be hard to prove that she would commit perjury herself."

Bessie was silenced. She knew that she was no match for the wily lawyer.

" I must again ask you to leave," Abel said tersely.

" This is my room," Daphne said, " and I am asking you to leave, Mr. Abel."

The lawyer's face contorted with naked rage, but his was a voice which never failed him. " You'll find I'm a bad man to cross, Miss Dixon," he warned. " I meant to do you the honour of asking you to become my wife. I am still ready to do so, but if you refuse to co-operate I shall certainly see to it that your brother is brought to justice and hanged, and that you go to the penitentiary for as many years as I can contrive to send you there."

He strode over to the door, slammed it, and was gone.

"Just look what a husband you might have gotten yourself," Bessie finally said with a half hysterical laugh, but Daphne didn't smile.

"I'm afraid of that man," she whispered.

"Don't ever think I ain't," Bessie said. "You—you won't weaken, will you?"

"About telling the truth? No. But it won't make any difference now. Nobody will believe me," Daphne said desolately.

"I wish Hondo was here," Bessie worried. "Maybe he would know what to—— What am I saying? The only thing to wish for is that both of them get away."

"Do you think they have a chance?" Daphne asked eagerly.

"With our help—maybe," Bessie answered. "Daphne, I think I know where they'll head for. It's that abandoned ranch where Willard was feeding the cattle. If we could meet them there we might find some way to help them hide, or get away."

"I'll do anything," Daphne declared.

"Then come with me."

They hurried across to Bessie's little white house, and Bessie drew down all the shades, but left one in the kitchen several inches from the sill.

"I've got to go over to the stable," she said. "Chances are this house is being watched. I'm going to start cooking something, but I'm going to turn the job over to you."

The air was soon redolent with the odour of frying pork chops and other good things. Bessie kept passing in front of the slightly raised window shade. Then she turned it over to Daphne, and quietly let herself out of the front door. As directed Daphne continued to pass in front of the window, and at times she pretended to be carrying on a conversation.

Bessie was back in twenty minutes. "I made it," she said, elated, "but just like I thought there is a man watching this window. We'll eat, talk a while, and then pretend to go to bed. I think he'll leave."

A little past midnight they left the house. Daphne was

wearing one of Bessie's riding costumes, and they were both warmly dressed.

They slipped furtively from the house, and took a roundabout way to the livery stable, which they approached from the rear. While Daphne remained outside on watch Bessie entered the rear door and exchanged a few words with Hank, the hostler. She came out leading two horses. Neither one wore a side-saddle. They mounted and rode away. When a mile out of town they stopped and listened. There was no sound that they were being followed.

Bessie was not too certain of the road. Several times she had to stop and take her bearings. A grey patch like the fur of a gigantic coyote was coming up in the east when they looked down upon a set of small ranch buildings nestled between a hillside banked with aspens, and the upper waters of a small river.

"Now if somebody don't take a shot at us we'll be all right," Bessie assured.

"You're sure they'll be here?" Daphne asked doubtfully.

"Almost certain. Hondo asked George A to send Spike Williams up here with supplies for Pat Young. It's perfectly natural then that Hondo should come here himself when he got away."

They rode slowly down to the buildings. There was no sign of life. They went into the house. Someone had been living there without doubt, but there was no one there now.

"This is where your brother spent the winter," Bessie murmured. "I was *sure* Hondo would come here. I still think he will."

"What had we better do?" Daphne wondered.

"Go back, I guess," Bessie said wearily.

They made themselves a cup of coffee. Finally Bessie said, "Well, I guess we'd as well get started."

"They might come yet," Daphne said. "Why not let me stay here just in case they do come?"

"Wouldn't you be scared?"

"Well, I've been scared before. I've nothing to go back for. I want to stay."

"Well, I suppose I should stay with you," Bessie said, "but if they are captured I'd like to be in town."

"You could send me word if anything happened," Daphne suggested.

"Yes, I could, and I will," Bessie said. "I wish I had brought my sixgun for you. I'd stay, but all the way out I've been thinking about what would happen if Hondo was caught and they raised a mob."

"I'll be quite all right," Daphne said. "You should go back. They'll miss you, but they won't me. If they happen to come in after dark I'll be here."

"You're not afraid?"

"Nervous, yes; but not afraid," Daphne answered with a strained smile.

She was still of that opinion when she watched Bessie ride over the hill, but to it was added a sudden lonesomeness. For the first time it occurred to her that not Hondo or Willard might appear, but some of her enemies.

Chapter XVIII — Caught in a Trap

Willard Dixon led the way into the sheriff's office after liberating Hondo and locking Ace Gillette in the vacated cell. George A. Kump was waiting uneasily in the sheriff's office.

"Well, Willard, I'm glad——" he said, and then stopped with popping eyes as he saw Hondo Horn right behind young Dixon. At the same time he noticed the gun in Willard's hand. "What—what does this mean?" he gasped.

"I let Hondo out, and we're leaving, Mr. Kump," Willard said.

"And I think it would look better if we tied you up, George A.," Hondo added pleasantly.

"This is damn' foolishness," Kump barked. "I put up bond for this kid to get him out of the country so his sister wouldn't have to perjure herself by testifying against you, but——"

"This isn't a case that can be solved with money, George A.," Hondo told his employer. "I appreciate you putting up all that dough, but it wouldn't do any good."

"And my sister wouldn't perjure herself to save me or her own skin either," Willard said proudly.

"But—but what can you do?" the bewildered banker mumbled.

"I'm not sure," Hondo said, as he began to tie his employer in the sheriff's chair. That finished he fished out a sixgun from the sheriff's desk.

Outside they found the two horses Kump had brought.

"I suppose you know this is as much of a surprise to me as it is to you," Hondo said.

"It was as little as I could do after the dirty trick I done you," Willard said with shame in his voice. "I didn't want to claim you give me that money."

"I never quite thought you did," Hondo said. "But now I want to know who actually did kill Tim Bell?"

"I don't know. It might've been any of 'em."

"Just who was in that poker game at the old prospector's cabin the night before Tim was killed?"

"You know about that?"

"Yes, for some time."

"There was the two Thornberrys, Tim Bell, Ozark, Lafe Lufkin, Brig Dow and me."

"Dow was there?" Hondo exclaimed. "The fellow who hopes to be sheriff. Did he know about Tim's murder?"

"He claimed he was the one who talked the Thornberrys into not having me arrested, but he knew all about it, all right."

"What happened?"

"I lost most of my summer's wages to Brig Dow before that night. I thought I might get it back from Bell when he showed up at the cabin with Ez and Rumel. I lost steadily, and finally I gave him my I O U for five hundred dollars.

"We played all night. After breakfast Tim said he was going to cut across the head of Swan Basin, and if he didn't see a buck he was going home. Then Ez told him to wait on the ridge, that the rest of us would beat the brush below and drive a buck up to him. We all scattered out, but I didn't see any buck. After while I heard a shot, and when I got to the ridge I met the whole bunch of them. They said Tim Bell was dead, and all of 'em but Dow swore they had seen me shoot him. That's all I know."

"You say you give Tim an I O U for five hundred. It wasn't found on him."

"They took it. I got pretty mad when they accused me but they had me covered. They took my gun away from me, and then they pretended to search me. Ez Thornberry claimed he got the I O U out of my pocket."

"And then they had you," Hondo said grimly. "They said if you didn't do everything they wanted they would accuse you of the murder."

"They sure drove it in, too. Do you remember a new red sweater I had?" Willard asked.

"Yes, I believe I do."

"They took that sweater away from me. They were going to claim the man they saw kill Bell wore a red sweater, and they said they would plant the sweater, with that I O U in the pocket of it where it could be found and identified as mine."

"That would explain why they didn't say they had seen Tim shot in the first place," Hondo said. "Pretty clever."

"Now," Willard said, "I'm going after that sweater."

"Hunh!" Hondo exclaimed.

"I'm not running away," the boy said. "They framed me, and I had to take it. But when they framed my sister, too, that was too damned much. I'm calling on the Thornberrys."

They were well along the road. Hondo had accepted his liberty for the sole purpose of going after his enemies, but he hadn't expected Willard to have the same thought. He wasn't exactly pleased.

"Look here, Willard," he said. "The trouble you've caused me ain't anything to what you've caused your sister. If you go snorting around after the Thornberrys you'll likely get yourself killed. When that happens they'll prove you killed Tim Bell, and break your sister's heart."

"You want me to run?" the boy asked incredulously.

"Just as fast as your legs will take you," Hondo said earnestly. "I'm involved in this, too. With you missing, but alive, they won't dare press their charges against me. With you dead they will—and prove it."

He wasn't in the least sure that he was right, but he was thinking of Daphne far more than himself. He meant to have things out with his foes himself, but he didn't want Willard Dixon along.

It took argument to convince Willard. They were still talking when they saw a horseman leading two pack horses through the sagebrush. They dipped into an arroyo and waited until the man passed, then they started to follow. Hondo knew it was Spike Williams on his way to Sep Kohler's place, but he didn't know how to make Spike know it was him.

They followed a couple of miles before a long finger of timber gave them a chance to overhaul the cowboy.

"Spike!" Hondo yelled. "Spike, this is me, Hondo."

The puncher stopped and grabbed at his gun. He thought it was Hondo's voice, but he knew that his foreman was in jail charged with murder.

Hondo called reassuring words, and rode out. Spike dropped his gun back in the holster with an exclamation of total bewilderment when he recognized his interceptors.

"How fur back's the posse?" he inquired.

"Not far," Hondo said. "Willard is takin' the packhorses from here."

"What's that skunk doin' out of jail anyway?" Spike blurted.

"Willard's all right," Hondo said. "He come clean. Took the blame, and then took Ace Gillette's gun away from him and broke me out."

Spike sized the young puncher up with new interest, but doubtful conviction.

"You go on to Kohler's place," Hondo directed Willard. "You'll find Pat Young there. That is you'll find him gone. You just make yourself at home, and if I know Pat you'll soon find yourself looking down his gun barrel."

Willard choked.

"There'll be no danger if you keep your head. I'll write a note for you to give Pat. Then the two of you head for the Upper Salmon River. Nobody will find you there. Then, the first time you get a chance, mail a letter back to Spike Williams telling him how you can be reached. Spike'll let you know how things stand," Hondo instructed.

Willard got under way without further argument.

"You're the damndest fool for a smart fellow I ever knew," Spike said frankly. "Lettin' that bird get away when you could have kept him here and cleared yourself."

"Ozark's murder has got nothing to do with that," Hondo said shortly. "This whole business has got to be cleared up. The kid would have stayed and helped me if I'd let him."

"I reckon you know the boys at the K Bar K will back you to the limit," Spike said.

"I know. All I want is for you to leave a little grub scattered around the range where I can find it. You might leave two or three good horses in the school section pasture where I could pick 'em up some night."

"So you're really takin' the hoot owl trail?" Spike queried dismally. "By Gawd, I'll gather the boys an' we'll wipe out the whole Thornberry gang."

"Stay out of it," Hondo said crisply. "You'll only get the old man into trouble, and interfere with me. Now get going. Chances are you'll find a posse at the ranch before you get back."

Hondo watched the puncher disappear on the back trail, then he turned and angled across the range toward Swan Creek.

He took his time, watching carefully for any sign of a posse. He felt strangely jubilant. His brief incarceration had once again reminded him of the joys of freedom. He remembered how he once heard a judge say, "Donald Horn, on account of your extreme youth, I am not meting out the penalty of life imprisonment which your accomplices have received, and taking into consideration the fact that you were not inside the bank when the cashier was killed, I now sentence you to ten years in the penitentiary."

Hondo had been innocent of the charge, and only Pat Young's squareness in giving himself up had saved him from being in prison right now.

He was not sorry that he had helped Pat, even though Pat had lied to him about being pardoned. He hoped Pat never would be taken. As for himself, having tasted imprisonment twice he didn't mean to taste it the third time.

It wasn't long after midnight when he came down a canyon little more than a mile above the Thornberry ranch. He tied his horse deep in a willow swamp and went on afoot until he could look down upon the scrubby buildings from behind the shelter of a clump of gnarled, snow-beaten aspens.

It wasn't the best hiding place in the world. He would have no chance of evasion if a posse came looking for him there. A keen-eyed man at the Thornberry place might see him if he happened to move at the wrong time. But it was the best he could do if he kept an eye on the place.

He was not surprised to see signs of activity at daybreak. The Thornberrys had breakfast early and caught up fresh horses.

Old Gus Marks was there, as well as Lafe Lufkin; and three more men arrived almost as soon as it was light. They were Heb Giles, Walk Thurgood, and a fellow from lower Swan

Creek called Dutchie. They were ready to ride, but were waiting for something.

It was just past sunup when a fast-riding horseman arrived. Hondo recognized Johnny Tebb, a young hoodlum from Highline, who occasionally rode the range for Brig Dow. Tebb got a fresh horse. Then, with the exception of old man Marks, they all rode away in the direction of Dow's place.

Hondo swore. He had expected the place to be left deserted. Old Gus Marks was a thief, and this had thrown him into the Thornberry crowd, but he wasn't the killer type. Hondo didn't want to hurt him. But he couldn't delay.

The party was scarcely out of sight before Marks came out of the cabin. The Thornberrys raised some hogs, and the old man began feeding them. Hondo had to manoeuvre carefully to reach the house unseen.

He started to search the house methodically, while at the same time keeping an eye on the door lest Marks catch him by surprise. There were three rooms, strung out in a row. He was half way through the first one when he heard Marks shuffling across the yard.

Hondo waited just inside the door until the old man came in. Things were not as they had been, and the man gave a surprised grunt.

"Have a chair, Gus," Hondo said as the man stepped further inside.

Marks grunted louder than before as he turned, but the sixgun pointed at him caused him to sit upon the nearest chair.

"Hondo Horn!" he breathed.

"Where did they go?" Hondo asked.

Marks hesitated, then seeing a flash of anger in Hondo's eyes, he answered, "Over to Brig Dow's. Brig's leadin' a posse."

"Why didn't Brig come here?"

"He stayed in town last night. Sent Johnny Tebb out to have the boys meet at his place."

Marks carried a sixgun. Hondo relieved him of it, examined the weapon, removed the cartridges and tossed it into the wood-box back of the stove. He made the old man go into the last bedroom, and tied him to a chair with strips torn from a filthy blanket.

A complete search failed to uncover the red sweater of the I O U which Hondo had hoped to find. He was keenly disappointed. There was but one other place where they were likely to be—inside Slick Abel's office.

Hondo faced the old man.

"You were here when I brought Ozark's body in. There was no powder marks on his undershirt then. Later there was. Somebody discharged a blank cartridge against it. Who was it?"

"I don't know, Hondo, honest I don't," the old scoundrel whined. "They made me go home right after you left."

Hondo decided that he might be telling the truth.

There had been a fire in the stove when Hondo first entered the house. He had put in a stick of wood, and set the coffee pot on to heat. Although he knew that his life was in danger every second he tarried he took time to fry a panful of eggs and wolf them down, abetted by the strong and acrid coffee. It might be a long time before he ate again.

He suddenly had cause to wish that he had gone hungry. He was sitting where he could keep an eye on the road. Just as he finished a ten-man posse broke into view. Without the least hesitation they turned up the short lane toward the Thornberry house.

Gus Marks' saddled horse stood in plain view by the stable, but Hondo couldn't reach it. In fact the instant he left the house he would be seen.

Chapter XIX — A Night of Terror

Daphne had hard work to keep from getting on her horse and following Bessie back to town. But staying here on the possible chance that the fugitives might slip in for supplies seemed the only way she might help them at all. She wanted desperately to talk to Willard just once more at least. And although she hated to acknowledge it to herself, she wanted to see Hondo again.

It wasn't so much that she might help them escape as it was that Hondo might want to send back some message. Bessie had been sure that he would.

She reasoned that although they might be close around they would be afraid to venture near in daylight. Even if they saw her from a distance they might think it some trick.

She didn't eat anything until nearly sundown, and then she climbed the hill for a final look around. It was deep dusk when she started back. She meant to sit up all night without a light.

She opened the cabin door, and a voice said, "Hello, sweetheart."

Daphne screamed, and jumped backward, but a long arm caught her wrist and jerked her forward. She felt her face against a coarse woollen shirt, then her face was tilted upward, and a mouth that smelled vilely of whisky and tobacco was pressed against her mouth.

Although she struggled desperately she was held as in a vice until the man had to pause to get his breath. She got one arm free then and struck him in the face. He only laughed, and caught both her wrists. The man was Rumel Thornberry.

"Waitin' for somebody, peaches?" he asked.

"I—I—got lost," she replied, and immediately wished that she hadn't said it.

"Now ain't it lucky I found you?" he laughed. "You an' me here all alone in this cabin all night——"

"Somebody will come,' she cried desperately.

Thornberry's face hardened. "I thought so," he said. "Waitin' for Hondo Horn and that punk of a brother to show up, hunh? That's just what I figgered."

"I didn't say that," she denied.

"Yuh didn't need to. Just you bein' here is enough."

He looked around the room and sniffed. She had cooked more food than she could eat. He sat her down roughly on a chair and wolfed down what looked to her to be fistfuls of food at a gulp.

She had no idea of the various evil intentions warring within him. That morning he had been riding on the extreme flank of the widely scattered posse led by Brig Dow. It happened he had been the only one to see Bessie Bell on her way back to Highline. She had been well past him, but he had turned and followed her a couple of miles before it dawned upon him that where she had come from was more important than where she was going.

Bessie had been careful to make sure that no one saw her leave town, but she had to take chances on being seen coming back.

By that time Rumel Thornberry had lost contact with his posse. He made a swift decision to back-track Bessie instead of following the others. It hadn't been hard to do, although it was slow business for eight or ten miles. By that time he was certain in his own mind that she had come from Sep Kohler's isolated ranch.

He recognized at once that it would be an ideal place for the fugitives to rendezvous with Bessie. He had made his approach circumspectly and with the utmost caution. He had been taken by surprise at sight of Daphne, but a slight fever had begun to rise in his blood. Still, he hadn't dared to move until absolutely certain that there was no one else around.

But she was certainly expecting somebody. For that reason, despite his wolfish desire to keep her in the cabin all night, he knew that it wasn't safe to do so.

"Come on, sweetheart," he said when he was through feeding, "I think we'd better change our quarters a little. I want to be on the outside when Hondo an' your brother get on the inside."

She tried to resist going with him, but a threat breathed into her ear caused her to desist. She went along dully, and obediently mounted her pony. He tied the reins firmly to the horn, then tied her hands behind her back. He led her pony out to where his own horse was hidden.

Daphne struggled desperately to free her hands as her mount followed behind Thornberry's, but it was impossible.

Darkness was upon them immediately, but he held the horses to a trot, which was hard upon Daphne because she couldn't use her hands.

At first he kept looking back, but gradually, as he busied himself with his own thoughts he looked around less often.

Daphne had no idea where she was being taken, but it was not toward town. They were in a timbered country of narrow, steep little canyons and ridges. She knew that Hondo believed Rumel Thornberry had been following her the previous Sunday when she came upon him and Pat Young working on Ozark, and now she believed him. She had never been so mortally afraid in all her life. She didn't even dare ask the man where he was taking her. But he suddenly volunteered that information.

"Slick Abel has got it into his head to marry you, I hear," he remarked. "I got an idee I can make it easier for him to get you—after while. But business before pleasure. I've got to get the boys an' pick up your friend Hondo an' the punk. But in the meantime I know of a sweet little place here in the hills where you'll be nice an' safe till I come back for you. I may even decide to marry you myself."

Lewd chuckles drifted back to her as the fellow let his imagination ramble. Daphne knew that she had to do something.

They crossed a small creek, and started up the side of a brushy sidehill. As they rounded a big sarvis bush Daphne threw her leg over the saddle horn, hesitated a moment, then dropped. Unable to keep her balance she fell forward on her face, but she had presence of mind enough to keep rolling.

The huge bush screened her from sight. She got her feet under her, started to run, stumbled over something and fell headlong, unable to catch herself because of her bound hands. The breath was knocked clear out of her and she could only lie where she had come to rest.

"Hey!" she heard Rumel yell a moment later, as he discovered his loss.

She heard him leap from his horse and come running back, the foulest language her shocked ears had ever heard pouring from his mouth like filthy water from a bung-hole.

Her breath came back, but she didn't dare move now. Fortunately, the impetus of her fall had driven her into a small patch of chaparral as if she had been a projectile. The roots had parted to let her down to the ground, while the sturdy, tangled green branches had closed over her like a protecting mantle. She couldn't have hidden herself half so well by a deliberate effort.

Thornberry stopped less than twenty feet from her. He had stopped cursing for a moment, but she could hear his angry breathing.

"You can't hide from me, you, you——" his tongue blasted out evil epithets. "I'll break your dirty little neck once I do get my hands on you."

He listened. He moved hastily down to the creek, then suddenly fearing that she might steal the horses he rushed back. He was still swearing, although in a lower key. There was worry as well as anger in his tone now.

He led the horses back to the creek and tied them, probably with knots so intricate that she would be fatally delayed if she tried to untie them with bound hands. Then he was silent.

Presently Daphne realized that she was actually straining her ears trying to hear him. Where was he ? How long would she have to stay there ? Once or twice she thought she heard something creeping on the other side of the chaparral, and for a moment she thought she would die. At any second he might pounce and drag her out. If he did she hoped that she might die.

Minutes that seemed eternities passed. She lay there on her stomach, not even daring to look up at the stars. Now the stiff, unyielding branches of the chaparral were gouging her in a hundred places, but she had to endure.

She believed that he was within a rod or so of where she lay, waiting, watching, listening. How long, she wondered, could she endure it ? She had to fight hard to keep down a rising sense of panic.

Then, quite without knowing how it happened, she found herself content to stay there. Her rigid body had relaxed. The branches still gouged, but not so painfully as before. It was like a runner getting his second wind. If necessary, she could stay there all night.

She didn't let her mind linger on the possibilities of what might happen after Rumel Thornberry went away. In fact she didn't think much of anything. Her mind had reached a crisis just a point short of hysteria, and the reaction had left it numb and inert.

She had no idea of how much time had passed when she heard Rumel again, and she realized that he had been standing right beside the big sarvisberry bush for a long time. The chaparral where she lay was well within his range of vision. He had thought there would be some sign if she was in there.

Rumel swore a mighty oath. " Well, anyway the damn' bears will get her before she finds her way out of here," he said, and she heard him marching down to his horses.

There was another agonizing ten minutes. She knew that he was waiting with a hope that his words would bring her out, crying for him to take her away. But no number of bears could ever frighten her as he had done.

Then she heard him mount his horse and ride away. But he didn't go on the way he had been going, nor did he go back the way he had come. He seemed to be travelling down the little creek.

Daphne waited as long as she thought she could stand it,

then dragged herself out of the chaparral. There was no moon, and scarcely any stars. Her face and hands were scratched, and there were numberless sore places on her body.

She still feared a trick. She was almost afraid to move lest her enemy suddenly pounce upon her from behind some bush or tree. But at last she forced herself to move toward the creek, but above the place where they had crossed it.

When she found the water she discovered that she had never been so thirsty in her life. She sprawled full length and plunged her lips into the water.

A quiver of stark terror shot through her as a sharp, penetrating wail rent the air not a stone's throw away. The sharp, jangling cadences continued for a full minute. By that time she knew that it was a coyote. The creature knew that she was there, and it was not afraid. But she was. She knew that coyotes never attacked humans, but this coyote might be an exception.

There was silence for a while, then the coyote gave three short, sharp yips from so close that Daphne was sure she could put her hand upon the creature—if she could only see it. A scream that outdid the coyote's best vocal efforts burst from her throat. She leaped the creek and started to run along the side of the ridge.

She was out of breath before she subdued her panic. That, she told herself, would never do. She had to be calm. She had no idea of direction. All the canyons they had crossed looked alike. She was sure only that she was going in the general direction of Sep Kohler's cabin.

She forced herself to walk slowly. She would have to wait until daybreak to get her bearings at all, but she must get far enough from the spot where she had lost Rumel Thornberry that she couldn't be found if the man returned later.

Twice more she heard the coyote yip, and she knew the animal was following her. However, she was no longer afraid of it. In fact she rather welcomed its company. What she feared most was that in the darkness she might suddenly meet a bear.

She paused at the root of a big pine tree to await daylight. It dawned finally, grey and sullen, with a hint of drizzling rain in the air. Visibility was limited to a few hundred yards. She had no idea which way to go. She was too cold to remain where she was, and with her hands tied behind her back she couldn't have started a fire even if she had had a match.

Daphne might have given way to panic then had she not already passed through a crisis which had forced her to exercise rigid control or face emotional collapse.

The clouds settled down wiping out all but the nearest trees, and what had promised to be a drizzle threatened to become a steady downpour. Her clothing was damp before she came to another clump of pines with boughs thick enough to shed most of the rain. Nothing remained except to settle down in damp and hungry discomfort to wait for the clouds to lift.

Chapter XX On the Heels of the Quarry

Deputy Sheriff Ace Gillette rode easily at the head of the advancing posse. Ace and Hondo had ridden range together for the K Bar K. They had been good friends. But Hondo knew that Ace would not allow friendship to interfere with duty. Ace would take him in, or stop a bullet.

Hondo's eyes hardened as he seized a butcher knife and cut old Gus Marks loose. " Listen to me, Gus," he said savagely. " There's a posse coming up the lane, and I won't be taken alive. You're going to stand in the door, and when that posse comes up you're going to tell them that there is nobody else on the place ; that everybody else has gone to look for Hondo Horn. I'll be standing just out of sight with this gun pointed at the coupling of your backbone. If you don't get 'em sent away I'll uncouple you with a bullet."

The old man paled, and his short chin-whiskers wagged nervously.

" Get hold of yourself if you want to live," Hondo warned ominously.

Marks moved silently to the door, while Hondo stationed himself no more than two feet to one side of him. The opening remark was not propitious.

" Hello, Gus, who you hidin' in there ? " Gillette greeted. Even Hondo couldn't be sure the remark was entirely facetious

" Huh—huh—what's that yuh say ? " Marks asked tremulously. His face, Hondo thought, must be a dead giveaway

" Never mind," Gillette said. " Where's the Thornberrys

" They gone out huntin' Hondo Horn," Marks said.

" Yeah ? Why ain't you out with 'em ? Cold feet ?

"I'd shore like to be," Marks said, speaking more truth than anyone except Hondo dreamed. "Ez asked me to stay here an' feed his hogs, an' kinda keep an eye on the place."

"Yeah, afraid Hondo Horn might show up here," said someone in the posse.

Hondo saw Marks give a visible start. The old man had to grip the door jambs with both hands to stay their quivering.

"Figgered it would be a good time to do a little lootin' while they were away, didn't you, Gus?" Gillette said. It was plain that Marks' reputation as a petty thief was what Gillette was thinking of mostly. But there was danger he might come inside to ascertain if Marks was trying to steal something.

"I'm tellin' yuh the truth," Marks argued shrilly. "If yuh don't believe me yuh just ask Ez or Rumel."

"I will," Gillette said shortly. "Where are they?"

"They left here for Dow's ranch. Then they was gonna cover the foothill along the Contacts."

"Let's not waste time with this old duffer, Ace," a posseman said impatiently.

"I guess that's right," the deputy said. "We'll ride through the narrows and cover Swan Basin, and if we don't find track of 'em there we'll cross the Contacts and probably meet up with Dow's outfit. Between us we'll have made a circle, and it's my idea Hondo will be somewhere inside it."

"Sheriff Watson thinks he'll be down on the breaks where Swan Crick empties into Rock River," a man said.

"If he is the sheriff 'll get him," Ace said.

"What about him hittin' into the Dugout Hills around Kohler's ranch?" another said. "That'll be just outside your circle."

"I've thought of that, but there's open country beyond," Gillette stated. "I'd be more inclined to think he'd try to catch a train out by Esmeralda than go that way."

They turned and rode away, but neither Hondo nor Marks moved until they had turned up the main road toward the Swan Basin narrows.

"You can set down now, Gus," Hondo said. It had been a close call, and he realized that his brow was covered with sweat. And Marks had been more frightened than he.

It had been a break, however, to learn where he was being hunted. Swan Basin had been the logical place for him to hide out, and Ace Gillette had been clever enough to guess it. The Contact Mountains, of which Swan Basin was a part, was a rough country that served the K Bar K as summer range. That, too, was a logical hiding-place. Hondo was glad that he had told Willard and Pat to cross the Dugout Hills to open country. He intended to leave enough sign around here that no posse would scan that country closely.

"Where at is yore pardner ?" Marks ventured to ask.

"Where do you think ?" Hondo snapped. "He's back here a ways watchin' our horses."

The old man's watery eyes sparkled cunningly.

Hondo tore more strips from the blanket and again tied Marks to a chair, and the chair to a bed. He estimated it would take Marks several hours to work himself loose. Before leaving he mounted the old man's horse, and rode it up to where he had left his own mount.

He had accomplished nothing. In any direction which he might choose to go there would be posses. He knew Ace Gillette well enough to know that the deputy lacked imagination. Ace had set his course and he would stick to it. Therefore, the safest place Hondo could think of was to follow the posse into Swan Basin.

He waited perhaps an hour, then kept to the timber until he reached Gus Marks' cabin. He stopped there long enough to unsaddle the old man's pony and turn it loose, then headed for the narrows. At the two places he had visited he collected a slicker, a blanket, and such emergency rations to last some three days in a pinch.

Getting entirely out of the country was the last thing he intended to do. He had failed in what he hoped to get. Now he had to strike hard, and strike sudden. And he would have to catch his foes unaware.

He felt better when he got through the dangerous narrows. An imaginative leader would have left someone to guard the narrows. It was easy to keep out of sight now.

He spent the night at the old prospector's cabin where Tim Bell had spent his last night on earth. It was cloudy in the morning so he ventured to build a fire. Soon it started to rain, and he remained inside the cabin.

It was well past noon when it stopped raining and the clouds began to clear away. He saddled his horse, tied his belongings on the back of his saddle, and rode away. It wouldn't do to remain too long in one place, and when Gus Marks' story was told somebody would guess his strategy. He had to keep moving. Had to keep following the tracks of the posse.

A two-hour climb brought him to a divide on the summit of the Contacts. He drew up to look around, and suddenly the sounds of rifle shots broke the silence. Listening carefully he soon made certain that the shots continued at intervals, and that they were rapidly coming his way.

Hondo spurred into the brush and waited; his horse's ears pricked ahead with eager interest. He heard the sobbing breath of a horse before the straining animal came into view. He recognized instantly a bay K Bar K horse. The rider was Pat Young!

Hondo spurred out of the brush, and sprang to the ground. His horse was practically fresh; those of the posse were sure to be winded when they reached the summit.

"What the hell——" Pat burst out as he stopped his all but exhausted mount.

"Take my horse," Hondo said. "Meet me later at the narrows."

"But——"

"Don't argue," Hondo snapped. "Where's Willard?"

"Branched off," Pat said as he transferred to the fresh horse. "The wallopers surprised us."

Hondo had no more than time to get the exhausted horse into the brush before the possemen came in sight. Ace Gillette was in lead. His horse was winded, and covered with lather, but in far better shape than the one Pat had been riding.

To Hondo's great concern Ace pulled up to wait for his men. If he looked closely enough the wet ground would betray the fact that two horsemen had just met there. However, the tracks made by Hondo's horse going back under Pat left a far clearer imprint, and Hondo hoped the others would not be noticed. He feared, though, that they might hear the palpitating breathing of the given out horse.

The remainder of the possemen arrived quickly. Some of the men Hondo had seen at Thornberry's were missing, but there were a few new faces.

"We'll split up," Gillette instructed. "Three of you men take the straightest way to the narrows. I'll follow his tracks; The rest of you fan out on each side. We oughta git him before dark."

"What about the other one?" somebody asked.

"Brig Dow's posse is behind us, they're sure to pick him up. Hondo Horn is the one we want anyway."

They dashed away. The tracks of that galloping horse going downhill were so plain that they hadn't even bothered to look around. Hondo smiled grimly. They thought that Pat was him. Gillette had recognized the K Bar K horse, but evidently hadn't got a good look at the rider.

He had little fear that they would overtake Pat Young now. Pat was well mounted, and he knew all the tricks. And Hondo had a greater worry. He understood that Pat had given Willard Dixon a chance to turn off, but they probably hadn't known about the other posse, composed entirely of Thornberry adherents. Once they got hold of the boy there was no telling what they might do.

He couldn't linger where he was. If the posse caught sight of Pat they would realize their mistake and come back. He let the horse rest for ten minutes, until it ceased to choke and gasp, then rode it slowly back the way it had come.

He might have known, he realized now, that Pat Young wouldn't run away and leave him in a hole. Willard, too, had wanted to stay and come to grips with his enemies.

He had promised to meet Pat at the narrows, but that could wait. Pat now had what food there was. If he eluded the posse he would conceal the horse somewhere and hide in the brush and rocks at the narrows until Hondo showed up.

His chances of finding Willard were also small. His deductions were that if the boy was caught they would proceed along the foot of the Contacts towards Swan Creek. They might, or might not pause at Brig Dow's rank on Wild Dog. Therefore, his best bet was to cut across the wildest part of the Contacts to Wild Dog Creek, and then try to ascertain if the Thornberry posse had crossed it.

He soon realized that he wasn't going to reach the Wild Dog before dark on his exhausted horse, but darkness nor daylight made any great difference to him now.

The sun had come out clear after the rain, but the air was still chilly. He came to a small mountain stream just before the sun set and the tired horse stuck its nose eagerly into the cold water.

Hondo's grey eyes suddenly bugged out with amazement. There, clearly defined in the mud, were the tracks of a woman's boot!

He leaped down to investigate. The woman had stopped to drink, then blundered on down the creek. She had no horse, and there were no other tracks.

They were small, delicate tracks, and the woman who made them was weary. Hondo saw where she had stumbled several times, and once where she had fallen on her face.

Whoever the woman was she was in trouble. She was lost. Had probably been lost in the storm, and when the fog had finally lifted had come upon this creek and had sense enough to follow its downward course. It was no business of Hondo's. Yet his humanitarian instincts revolted against leaving a woman in distress. Her tracks were fresh. She was miles from the nearest habitation, in the wildest section of the entire range.

He fought the issue out silently, then raised his voice in a loud yell. There was no answer. He yelled again and again as he followed down the stream. Finally he took out his gun and fired two shots in rapid succession. No answer.

He holstered the gun and urged the now somewhat refreshed horse to a faster walk. He yelled again, but with little hope that he would get an answer. He knew that lost people frequently lost their wits. The woman might actually hide from him.

And he was acutely aware that his shots and yells would be disastrous indeed if they happened to be heard by his enemies.

Suddenly he heard his own name spoken by a small, frightened, and very weak voice. He jerked about abruptly. The woman had crossed the creek, and hidden in the brush on the other side until he had passed by.

" Daphne ! " he exclaimed. " What in the devil are you doing here ? "

She tried to explain, but a moment later she was sobbing against his breast. He saw that her hands were tied behind her back.

CHAPTER XXI HONDO HEARS BAD NEWS

HONDO caressed the girl's hair gently while he let her break the strain she had been under with tears. He got out his knife as soon as her trembling subsided a little, and turned her gently around.

" I'm quite all right now," she said.

" Then hold still while I cut these thongs."

He cursed under his breath when he got a good look at her wrists. Even though the thongs had not dug into her flesh deeply at first they were tight enough to cut and bruise the tender skin as her wrists began to swell. It was a ticklish job cutting the thongs without also cutting the flesh.

" Who did it ? " he breathed.

" Rumel Thornberry."

Hondo said nothing. One more score to be chalked up against that hateful enemy, he thought grimly.

" I was scared to death when I heard you call out and shoot," Daphne confessed. " I—I tried to hide."

" But why ? You were lost, wasn't you ? "

" Yes, but I was afraid it might be someone else. I never dreamed that it could be you. I called as soon as I recognized you."

" Not so long since I'd have been about the last person you would have trusted," he reminded smilingly. " I'm glad you're not afraid of me."

" Where is Willard ? " she whispered.

" He should be safe now," he said thoughtfully. " I sent him to Sep Kohler's place to find Pat Young, and told 'em both to get out of the country while the posse was hunting me. But tell me what you're doing here ? How did you get lost ? How long have you been here ? "

" Since last night," she answered the last question first. " I escaped from Rumel Thornberry as he was taking me somewhere."

Hondo took her by the shoulders and looked at her. Her quiet words didn't fool him about the ordeal she must have gone through.

" Where did you fall in with Rumel Thornberry ? " he asked.

He had her sit down while she told everything from the time she had gone to Bessie Bell's house.

Hondo understood now how Pat and Willard had been routed out of their hiding-place in the Dugout Hills. He guessed that the two riders had left the Kohler place on some mission of their own before Daphne and Bessie had arrived there, and had returned later, just in time to be almost picked up by their enemies after Rumel Thornberry had returned with Dow and the others after losing Daphne in the mountains. The girl had been twenty-four hours without food, she had endured a long cold rain, the terror of being lost, and perhaps worst of all the fear of being recaptured by Rumel Thornberry. She didn't tell him what Rumel had said to her, but he could guess. It was a wonder she was not in a state of complete collapse. She was showing splendid courage, but he sensed that another night in the wilds would have surely broken her down.

One thing he knew. He must get her back to town. At once.

He put her on Pat's horse, and led the animal down out of the mountains. He joked her a little about not trying to pull the stunt on him she had pulled on Rumel, but they soon lapsed into silence.

Now and then he asked her if she wanted to rest, but each time she said she was all right. He wasn't used to walking, and his boots began to wear blisters on his heels, but he didn't mention it.

" You're not taking me back to Highline ? " she asked once.

" Sure thing. Can't leave you out here."

" But you'll be caught," she protested.

" I rather wanted to go back anyway."

" You're going to give yourself up ? "

" That," he said, " will depend on circumstances."

Highline lay peacefully quiet when they approached it at two o'clock in the morning. The tired horse, sensing food and rest at last, quickened its pace. They stopped at the rear of Bessie's livery stable, and Hondo helped Daphne down.

" Don't go to the hotel," he instructed. " Go to Bessie's place and stay there, but tell Bessie to come here at once."

Daphne wondered at the quick stab of jealousy that struck at her heart. Bessie loved this man, and when he was in trouble Bessie was the one he turned to. Daphne knew that she had no claim on him at all, and yet she wanted, with all the desire that was in her to do something for him. She trod wearily and stiffly over to Bessie's little white house, and remembering Bessie's caution went around to the window of the young widow's bedroom and knocked on the glass.

A moment later she saw Bessie's face at one side of the window. "This is Daphne," she said.

Bessie gave a sort of bleat, then told her to come to the rear door.

"Where on earth did you come from?" Bessie demanded as she drew her inside. "Where have you been? I'll draw the blinds, then light a lamp."

The lamp revealed Bessie in a white muslin nightdress that swept the floor. Her hair was in curl papers.

"Sit down, child," she cried as she looked at Daphne's face. "My heavens, you look as if you'd been through a thrashing machine. What happened?"

"Quite a lot," Daphne answered. "Hondo is waiting for you at the livery stable."

"Hondo? Here?"

"He brought me in. I was lost in the mountains since last night. He found me."

"He shouldn't be here. Every man in the county, almost, is looking for him. Public feeling is a hundred times as strong against him now since they claim he murdered old Gus Marks."

"What?" Daphne gasped.

"Never mind. I must throw a dress on and go see him." Bessie hesitated a moment. "When did you eat?" she asked.

"About thirty hours ago, but never mind that," Daphne said. "Just let me lie down some place."

"Go ahead. I'll start a fire, and if you feel able you can get yourself something."

Bessie was rushing away to the man she loved. Daphne couldn't blame her, but it made her feel strangely despondent.

Hondo had awakened Hank, the hostler, as soon as Daphne left. The man had grumblingly opened the door, then almost dropped his lantern as he saw who it was.

"Ganders!" he exploded. "What you doin' here?"

"Never mind," Hondo said. "Take care of this horse. I've sent for Bessie."

He wasn't afraid of Hank betraying him, for the man was utterly loyal to Bessie.

A few minutes later Bessie slipped in by the back door. "Hondo!" she whispered, and seized both his hands.

Hondo kissed her.

" You fool," she said bitterly, " you risked your life to bring little Red Riding Hood in out of the woods."

" She had a hard time. Rumel Thornberry saw you coming back and followed your tracks to Kohler's. He caught Daphne while she was waiting for me and Willard to show up, and started to take her into the Contacts to hold her some place till he rounded up his gang and got me. She got away from him, but has been lost in the dark and the rain ever since."

" I know," Bessie sighed. " And your life doesn't mean a thing compared to getting her back safe. Do you know they're saying you murdered old Gus Marks ? "

That was a shock Hondo hadn't expected. " Was he found tied up in a chair ? " he asked.

" And with his brains blowed out with his own gun. Slick Abel found him. He went out there, he claims, to see Ez Thornberry. He found Marks dead. The house had been ransacked, Marks' gun was in the wood-box, and Ace Gillette says now he was sure you were in the house when the posse stopped there and talked to Marks."

" I was. I had a gun on him."

" Oh, Hondo, you won't have a Chinaman's chance if they catch you now. What are you going to do ? " Bessie moaned.

" I intend to get something out of Slick Abel's safe that I'd hoped to find at Thornberry's. It's more important now than it was before. Slick Abel himself killed poor old Marks. It's time that skunk met up with a bullet. "

" I know that. But that don't mean you should ram your neck into a noose until you have to," practical Bessie declared. " You take the best horse in this stable and clear out."

" Any horse of yours would be missed, and the one I brought in is give out. What chance would I have keeping out of the way of all these posses ? "

" Then what *will* you do ? "

" I know all about how Tim was killed," he replied. " The Dixon kid was framed. If I can get hold of a red sweater and a five hundred dollar I O U that I believe is in Abel's office then I can afford to stand trial for killing Ozark."

" But not for killing Gus Marks," Bessie reminded.

" I'll admit that's a tough break, but I'll have to face that when the time comes. The whole thing hinges on them not being able to hang Tim's murder on to the Dixon kid," he said.

" It all hinges on you having gone hay-wire about the Dixon kid's sister," Bessie stated positively.

Hondo reached into a sack and hurled a handful of oats against the wall. "Don't be crazy," he said half angrily. "It's my own neck I'm thinking about."

"It won't be worth a dime if you're caught. The Thornberrys will raise a mob to lynch you."

"What do you know about Slick's habits?" Hondo queried.

"He sleeps in a room back of his offices. As you know the stair door leading from the street is always locked about midnight, and nobody gets up there without a pass-key. Try to jimmy that door and the night marshal would be sure to see you."

"Then I guess I'll have to wait till to-morrow night."

"Where?"

"Here, I thought."

Bessie studied a moment. "What about the horse?" she asked.

"Pat Young was riding it. I'm worried about Pat or Willard being caught, especially Willard. Daphne can explain the horse. She was lost. She found the horse abandoned, caught it and came home. Meanwhile, I hide in your store."

"It might work," Bessie said doubtfully. "Just possibly. I can coach Hank. But I'm afraid the sheriff will search everything, even my house."

"I think I can fix it—with Hank's help," Hondo said. "You've got a lot of grain in the back of the feed store. We can take some sacks out of the middle, cover the hole over with boards. I'll crawl in, and Hank can cover me over with sacks."

"It's better than anything I can think of," Bessie admitted. "We'll get Hank, and while you're doing that I'll go back and get you something to eat. I'd better feed Daphne, too."

"You're a darling, Bessie," Hondo grinned at her.

It was almost daybreak before Hondo crawled into a not too comfortable space long enough for him to lie upon a pile of horse blankets, or to kneel, but not high enough to stand upright. He had a jug of water and some sandwiches, and his sixgun. He sat back on his haunches while Hank toiled to cover him over.

"Can you hear us?" Bessie queried at last.

Her voice sounded a little remote, but he answered that he could.

"There's not a sign of you being there," she said. "I'll see you to-night."

"Don't worry about me, Bessie," he called. "The only danger is I may snore."

He composed himself to sleep. He had need of it. He had no sense of time at all when he was awakened by voices. He rolled up on his knees to listen.

He recognized the gruff, growling tones of Sheriff John Watson. "I like you as a woman, Bessie," he said, "but I think you're the damndest liar on earth when you say you don't know where Hondo Horn is."

"Now wait a minute, Sheriff," Bessie said. "Before you go to tearing my place of business upside down let's get things straight."

They had stopped as near to Hondo as they could possibly get and it was Bessie who had done the stopping. Hondo knew that she must have a reason.

"All right, Bessie, speak your piece," the sheriff said.

"Up to now I admit that I thought Hondo was all right, but now that I've read the poor Dixon kid's confession, and know that Hondo Horn knew all along that he had murdered my husband, that makes things a heap different. Hondo made him steal those cattle, maybe he even paid him to murder Tim," Bessie said with well-simulated bitterness.

"God knows I've been fooled plenty by Hondo Horn myself, but why would he do that?" the sheriff asked.

"I'm not exactly a poor woman, Sheriff, and Hondo Horn has asked me to marry him."

Sheriff Watson might have seen some grain sacks wiggle mysteriously had he happened to look in the right direction. Hondo Horn had bumped his head upon the boards above him.

"Then he's even lower than I thought," the sheriff ground out. "I know he served time, and that he protected an escaped life termer."

"What I hate most," Bessie said, "is that poor Dixon kid getting killed after he had confessed. There couldn't be anything phony about that, could there, Sheriff?"

Hondo pressed his ear against the sacks so as not to miss a word, but his worst fears had been realized.

"How do I know?" Watson barked. "All I know is Brig Dow has made me look like a fool. He catches young Dixon, after I've failed to catch anybody. Then he forces him to make a complete confession. Then, when the kid makes a break for liberty Dow kills him."

"That wouldn't be murder, would it?"

"No. I had to swear Dow in as a special deputy myself."

"And the confession itself couldn't have been forced?"

"It undoubtedly was. If it hadn't been for the corroborating evidence of that sweater and I O U I'd doubt the truth of it. But his own sister identified his handwriting. They may have got it under duress, and then shot the kid to keep it from being known, but we'll never be able to prove it."

"Well, anyway, Sheriff, you know now why I wouldn't protect Hondo Horn," Bessie said. "And if he had come here with Daphne don't you suppose that she would admit it now?"

"I guess you're right, but there's no understandin' women," Watson said gloomily.

They walked back to the front of the building, and Hondo wilted on to the horse blankets. He wanted out of that self-made dungeon. He had never before felt such blind, consuming hate. He knew what had happened. Brig Dow and the Thornberrys had captured Willard Dixon. They must have convinced him that they held his sister a prisoner, and that terrible things would happen to her unless he signed a lying confession of murder. They had probably given him a chance to try to escape so that they could kill him, but they would never have allowed him to reach town alive under any circumstances.

In their determination to get control of the county so that they could wreck the K Bar K and anyone else that might yield them a profit, Slick Abel and his minions had already committed four cold-blooded murders, and if Hondo was caught he would be the fifth victim.

Only one thing prevented him from tearing his way out of there right now and going on a rampage to kill as many of his foes as he could before they downed him. Two things rather. One was the remarkable faith of Bessie Bell and Daphne Dixon. The other was that he still held one card up his sleeve which might be used to expose the chief conspirator.

Chapter XXII A False Rumour

Daphne had been sitting by Bessie's window just before noon when she saw a number of horsemen riding slowly and solemnly up the main street of Highline. Her eyes focused instantly upon the body of a man tied face downward across a saddle, just as she had once seen the man Ozark tied. All she could see was the man's legs, but it was enough. A shrill cry of grief escaped her lips. Then all the colour drained from her face, and she stared at the gruesome parade with eyes dilated by horror.

"Willard!" her cold lips uttered.

She saw Bessie come out on the steps of the feed store as the men passed. Rumel Thornberry, the man she had plenty of reason to hate, stopped and exchanged a few words with Bessie. Then he spurred up to join the others.

A minute later Bessie came running across the street to her home.

"Daphne, did you see——" she asked.

"I saw. It was Willard. They killed him."

"Getting both barrels at once won't hurt any more than one at a time," Bessie said. "Somehow, they forced him to make a confession that he did kill my husband after all. And they've produced the evidence Hondo risked his life to try to find."

Daphne got to her feet, although she swayed dizzily. "I'm going to tell the sheriff about that man taking me into the hills," she said.

"No, wait. It can't do any good. Don't you see: Rumel will only claim he was taking you to a safe place so you couldn't interfere with them capturing Hondo and Willard. He's in the clear. Things that can't do you any good had better be kept to yourself."

"I suppose you're right," Daphne said.

"Here's what I want to know," Bessie said grimly. "This confession of your brother's is going to make it look like Hondo was the dirtiest crook that ever lived. Are you going to weaken and tell the officers where he is?"

Daphne met the other woman's eyes squarely. "I never will," she stated simply.

" That's all I wanted to know," Bessie said.

Daphne had already been interrogated by the sheriff about the horse, and she had stuck to her story. Later in the day the sheriff had visited her again. He was accompanied by Brig Dow, who already acted as if he were sheriff elect.

They showed her the bottom of a folded paper containing Willard's signature. She admitted that it was his. Then they showed her more writing, which she also had to admit was Willard's. Then they allowed her to read his complete confession.

" Now, if you have been protecting Hondo Horn in any way, miss, it's your duty to tell us all that you know," Watson said.

" I've already told you everything," she said. " I don't believe this confession. Willard was forced to write it, and then he was murdered."

" I shot him myself," Dow yelled. " You dare accuse me of murder ? "

" Yes."

" By Gawd——"

" Shut up, Dow. I'm *still* sheriff," Watson said. " I might be inclined to agree with you, miss, if it wasn't for one thing. The confession states that he was wearing a red sweater when he killed Tim Bell. He says that after he killed Bell he took an I O U for five hundred dollars away from him and hastily stuck it in the pocket of the sweater.

" Then, for fear he might have been seen, he took off the sweater and hid it under the grain-box at the K Bar K ranch, and forgot to remove the I O U. We found the sweater with his I O U to Tim Bell right where it said in this paper it would be."

" I still don't believe it," Daphne said. " My brother was framed."

Only a few minutes after they had left Slick Abel called. Daphne didn't want to see the man, but she was alone in the house, and she knew she had to have it out with him. She met him at the door.

" Well, aren't you going to let me come in ? " he said angrily.

" Mrs. Bell is not at home. I have no right to admit anyone," Daphne said.

" Bosh ! She's looking this way right now, and I've *got* to see you. Alone."

" You are no longer my attorney."

"So that's the way it stacks up. You're going to play with fire. It looks like you had seen enough to know how dangerous that is."

"I know that you and the Thornberrys will not stop at anything."

"I'm glad you recognize that fact," he snarled. "Now get this: I don't know what your brother told you, but if you say anything, anything, mind you, that might tend to contradict that confession then I'll accuse you of bribing a witness, and conspiring to defeat justice. We don't care whether we connect Hondo Horn with cattle stealing or not now that we've got him hooked for murder. And no wild story that you could possibly tell would be believed."

"Is that all, Mr. Abel?" she asked.

"That's all. I want my answer now. Keep still, and you'll be all right. But if I don't get your promise then I'll hand over Bill Burgess's affidavit that you paid him a thousand dollars to swear to a lie, to the prosecuting attorney. Burgess will back it up."

"I'm going to tell the entire truth, Mr. Abel, if I do have to go to the penitentiary," she stated calmly.

Abel stared at her in exasperation. "You're a crazy little fool," he told her bluntly, and turned away.

Daphne had not yet been able to bring herself to look at Willard's body. Despite Bessie's kindness she felt utterly friendless and alone. She knew that Bessie was in love with Hondo Horn. But, quite against her will, Daphne loved him, too. She was sure that Bessie was quite well aware of it, even though Hondo wasn't. It was a bar between her and Bessie and always would be.

She felt a warm surge of gratitude therefore when old George A. Kump knocked at the door, and spoke to her with fatherly friendliness.

"You ain't been over to see your brother's body," he said. "Would you like me to go over with you, Daphne?"

"Oh, I would," she said gladly. "Please come in a minute."

"Good job you and Bessie are doin' hidin' out Hondo," he said casually.

She glanced at him quickly. "You know——"

He chuckled slightly. "I do now," he said. "Bessie denied it. It's all right. I was sure of it anyway."

"Hondo isn't guilty," she asserted. "Neither was my

brother a murderer, even if they did force him to say he was. He thought I was their prisoner, and I was for a time."

"Tell me," he ordered.

Daphne poured out her story. She felt perfectly sure now that she could trust this homely old man.

"When Rumel took you away from the Kohler cabin," he said when she had finished, "did you leave anything behind you?"

"Why, yes. My handbag. I remember now. I guess I've been too excited to think about it."

"I guess that accounts for it. Was there anything else?"

"Yes. I had some things wrapped inside a coat on the back of my saddle—things that Willard would know were mine."

"The poor kid," George A. said. "He was sure they had you, and they made him believe doing what he did was the only thing would save you."

"He gave his life for me," Daphne sobbed.

"You should be very proud of him," Kump said. "There was better stuff in him after all than any of us realized. He could have got clear away if he had wanted to, or if he had done what I wanted him to."

Daphne felt better after her talk with George A. She was able to look at Willard without losing her composure. George A. accompanied her back to Bessie's house. On the way they met Harold Thatcher, the bespectacled young country attorney. He bowed, somewhat formally. Daphne wondered if he already had signed a warrant for her arrest.

"Now don't you worry," Kump told her at the door. "I'm for you all the way, and I've still got some influence in this county. People who go as far as Abel and the Thornberrys have done always overreach themselves."

She felt better than she had for some time. She had supper prepared when Bessie finally came home from the store.

"I see you've been busy with callers," Bessie said, as she hung up her things.

"Mr. Kump was very nice, but I'm afraid he knows about Hondo," Daphne said. "I didn't mean to——"

"Did you let anything slip to any of the others?" Bessie asked sharply.

"I swear I didn't. And Mr. Kump said he already knew."

"Well, I guess he did all right. He's no fool. He won't give Hondo away."

"But what will he do?" Daphne asked anxiously. "He can't stay hidden in your store forever."

"What I'm worried about is that he won't stay there long enough. I had to lock up at closing time. They'd have been suspicious if I hadn't."

They were almost through the meal when excitement in the street took them to the window. Somebody on a horse was yelling and making excited gesticulations in front of the Senate Saloon. Men were running out to their horses and mounting.

They watched uneasily while a posse numbering well over twenty men dashed out of town. Sheriff Watson was with them. The posse had scarcely vanished from sight when George A. Kump came over from the hotel.

"What is it? What's happened?" Bessie demanded.

"It's some kind of a hoax. Johnny Tebb just came in with word that Hondo had positively been seen down by the mouth of Swan Crick. We know where he is, and I think they do."

"You think it's a trick to get us to try to get Hondo away while the posse is out of town?" Bessie asked.

"I think so."

"Then we've got to warn him. He may try to escape any time."

"If one of us goes over there, and the place is watched they'll know he's there," George A. pointed out. "Our hands are tied."

"Were the Thornberrys in that posse?" Bessie asked.

"No. For some reason they pulled out quite a while ago. Even Brig Dow."

"Then I know it's a trick," Bessie said. "Hondo must not leave that store to-night."

"But suppose they have guessed where he is, and this is only to get the sheriff and his men out of town so they can kill him?" Daphne put in.

Both of the others turned to stare at her.

"It could be either one," Kump said. "He may be killed if he stays, and he may be murdered if he tries to leave. Dammit, I'm getting old. I don't think fast any more. You girls sit tight. I've got a ride to make. In a hurry. I've got to get my boys back here."

But George A. didn't know that his crew had already heard the false news, and were on their way to the mouth of Swan Creek, hoping to help Hondo.

CHAPTER XXIII "GIVE 'EM HELL"

HONDO swallowed the last of his sandwiches, took a final draught from the water jug, and composed himself to wait for Bessie to close the feed store. Within five minutes after he heard her leave he began to push and heave, and presently he emerged from the pile of grain sacks like a squirrel coming out of its den.

It was only dusk outside, but within lamps would have been lighted had there been customers. He was in time to see Johnny Tebb arrive, and to see the posse leave town in a great hurry a few minutes later.

He knew that Willard was dead. It occurred to him that the law had struck Pat Young's trail once again. But he wasn't long in figuring out the same possibilities that his friends across the street had foreseen. There wasn't much use trying to carry out his original plan, now that Willard's red sweater with the I O U had been located. He still thought it must have been hidden in Abel's office until very recently, when it had been surreptitiously transferred to the K Bar K ranch.

His presence in Highline was a constant menace to his few remaining friends. He must get out of town, and then commence the lone wolf warfare against his enemies which now he wished he had started long ago.

The store was locked, but there was a connecting door into the livery stable which he could open from his side. But he knew that Hank wasn't alone in there.

He moved near enough to the windows in the front to get a view of the street, and he saw George A. walking rapidly toward the livery stable. He half expected his employer to unlock the connecting door, but instead he heard George A. loudly order Hank to saddle his horse. A few minutes later George A. galloped away in the direction the posse had taken.

Hondo wished that he could have a word with Hank, but that wouldn't do. He had a convincing hunch that every move Hank made was being watched. There were two other doors, front and back, by which he could leave, since all of them had spring locks. The front door was out of the question, and he felt certain that both of the others were being watched.

In any event there would be little use for him to leave without a horse. It would be better to wait until after midnight. He prowled about the feed store nervously for perhaps an hour. Waiting was going to be hard. Then, suddenly, he began to sniff. It was a few minutes before he realized what it was. Smoke. Smoke that carried the odour of burning hay! And it was coming from the loft of Bessie's livery stable!

For a moment he felt a ghastly weakness in his stomach. If the dry hay in the loft was on fire both buildings would burn. Nothing could save them. And there were at least forty horses in the lower part of the barn that must be got out at once or they would be destroyed.

There was no use for him to remain in hiding and be burned to death. He flung open the connecting door and emerged into the harness room. He closed the door behind him after cocking the spring lock back.

"Hank!" he shouted. "Where are you?"

Hank, followed by two other men, rushed out of the office where he slept on a cot. His lantern was in his hand.

"It's Horn!" one of the men yelled.

"Shut up!" Hondo snapped. "The hay loft is on fire. We've got to get the horses out"

"Ganders!" Hank cried, appalled. "I thought I smelled somethin'. Crackies! Lemme open the door."

"No," Hondo forbade. "We must use the back door. Leave the front door shut. It would make a draught. Get busy."

He himself rushed up the stairs, and a blast of heat drove him back. Once started, the fire had swept from one end of the loft to the other in a minute. It would only be a minute or so at most before the fire would be seen from the street. The important thing now was to get as many of the horses out as possible. The animals had already smelt the smoke and fire. They were leaping about in their stalls, and some of them were starting to squeal.

Hank, an experienced horseman, was already getting some of the animals outside, but the two men with him had disappeared—probably to spread the word that Hondo Horn had been hiding in the livery stable and had set fire to it.

Hondo went to work with the horses nearest the front end—those which would have to be moved farthest. It was hard to get the animals started, and he had to watch that he didn't get kicked.

By the time he had three or four animals out it was light as day inside. There was a dull, hissing roar from overhead, and Hondo could hear the excited cries of people outside in the street.

Then, as he made his third trip to the back door he bumped against another man coming back in. At first he thought it was Hank, but remembered that Hank was behind him. He looked around, and the other man did, too. It was Ace Gillette.

"Figgered you were hid up in here some place," Gillette said. "Damn careless with your cigarettes."

"Come on, let's get out some more horses," Hondo said.

"Don't try gettin' away," Gillette warned. "I arrest you for murder."

"To hell with you," Hondo said. He dashed back, and began untying horses. But now the smoke was stifling.

"I'll turn 'em out of the stalls, Ace—you an' Hank keep 'em moving," he yelled.

He worked fast, aware that at any moment the ceiling joists might give way, and the whole top of the building come tumbling in.

His mind wasn't altogether occupied with getting out the horses. He wanted to get away. He knew that Ace Gillette would shoot him in an instant if he tried anythng.

As he loosened the last horse he saw the front joists start to sag.

"Look out, Hondo!" he heard Ace yell. "The roof's falling in."

Hondo turned and ran straight back under the falling roof.

Just as the roof collapsed Hondo dived into the harness room. There was a roof of thin boards over this and the office in front. For a moment it sustained the weight of the sagging timbers and such hay as had not yet been consumed, and then it, too, collapsed. But not before Hondo had got through the connecting door into the feed store.

His lungs were full of smoke, but he staggered back toward the rear of the building. The feed store was on fire from the outside, and it was full of smoke, but the flames hadn't yet reached the interior. Luckily, he found the rear door and staggered outside just as the rest of the roof started to fall in. The crowd at the rear of the stable at the moment had turned their backs to run, and nobody saw him emerge. They were to the right of him, and he staggered to his left.

He struck the corral fence, and fairly fell over it, and lay there in comparative darkness. As soon as he could begin to breathe again he crawled farther into the enveloping darkness.

He heard a man yell, " Hondo Horn was in there. I saw the roof fall on him ! "

Hondo smiled. They thought he was dead ! If he could keep out of sight for a while he would be safe.

He still needed a horse. Then he remembered. Ace Gillette had been at the fire. Ace always kept two good horses in a barn not far from the courthouse, on the other side of the town. He made a wide circle and cautiously approached the stable. The horses were there, the freshest one saddled for an emergency. Hondo led the animal outside, mounted, and Highline was soon left behind him. He was rather pleased to find Gillette's carbine in a scabbard underneath the fender.

The pure air of the mountains had never been so sweet as it was now. He had never valued freedom more highly. It wouldn't last long, but for the next few hours Hondo Horn intended to *live*.

He took the same route he had once taken with the hospital herd to reach the Swan Creek narrows. Once there he gave a whistle that sounded like, " OOh-wee-hoo." It was an old signal he and Pat Young had used as kids. At the third repetition it was answered. Pat came clambering down from among the rocks.

" Well, I don't see how you made it," Pat said after they had shaken hands, " but you must've."

" Your horse close around ? " Hondo asked.

" Maybe half a mile. We goin' somewhere ? "

" Depends. You've got a good chance to get out of the country. I've got a job to do." Hondo related the things that had happened since their weird meeting on the summit of the Contacts.

" This looks like the kind of job I like," Pat said. " I won't be in a damn' bit more danger after it's over than I am now. If I smack up against a bullet, well, that's bound to come sooner or later." He finished with a shrug.

" I don't know quite what they're trying to do," Hondo said, " but they think I'm dead. I don't believe they went on that wild-goose chase they sent the sheriff on. They're probably home in bed. But we can be there when they get up."

" What're we waitin' for ? " Pat asked.

They made their approach to the Thornberry place by the same route Hondo had used when he talked to Gus Marks, and left their horses in the same place. They hadn't much time. When Ace Gillette missed his horse he would know that Hondo had escaped from the burning barn. Hondo could only hope Ace wouldn't discover his loss before morning.

They approached warily. Hondo carrying Ace's carbine. Their first reconnaissance revealed a complete dearth of horses and saddles.

"They're out," Pat said. "And we're in. Wonder if they'll give us time to cook supper? I could stand a hot cup of coffee."

"I'm afraid not," Hondo said. "Stand guard, while I take a look inside."

He had just gone outside when Pat said, "Listen: ain't them wagins?"

Hondo bent an ear, and he could hear the chuckling sound made by several slow moving wagons. He emitted a low whistle.

"What's it mean?" Pat queried.

"Oats," Hondo said softly. "They sent the sheriff chasing away down to Rock River after me, and naturally all the boys at the ranch went along, probably to see if they couldn't give me a hand. Then they took their wagons and went down to haul back those oats we got back for Bessie."

"There'll be more than three of them then," Pat said thoughtfully.

"Five wagons at least, and from six to ten men," Hondo said.

"What the hell, there are two of us," Pat said recklessly, and his words echoed what was in Hondo's mind.

Hondo had waited long enough. Time meant everything now.

"We'll wait till they group up around that granary," he said. "You stay behind the shop, and I'll take the barn."

They heard the loaded wagons rumbling up the short lane. There were six of them, and two men on horseback riding ahead. Eight men in all.

The two horsemen came directly to the stable and tied their horses inside. Hondo was directly behind the stable, beside the open hay window. He could hear everything they said.

"We won't unsaddle," he heard Rumel Thornberry say, "but I don't look for any more trouble now that Hondo Horn, damn him, is dead."

"Boy, he must have fried some here before he started fryin'

in hell," Lafe Lufkin laughed. " An' the beauty of it is everybody thinks he started the fire."

" You're sure nobody saw you ? "

" Hell, no. I was right up to the edge of the crowd when the feed store started to burn, but nobody noticed me," Lufkin boasted.

Rumel Thornberry chuckled. " I wonder if Bessie carried insurance ? "

" Guess I better give these nags a forkful of hay," Lufkin said, and climbed over the manger and through the window.

No sooner did his head come through than Hondo struck viciously with the barrel of his sixgun. Lufkin emitted a shuddering sound, but Hondo seized him with the other hand and dragged him on through.

" What's the matter ? " Rumel asked.

" Nothin'," Hondo answered, disguising his voice as much as he could. He grabbed a pitchfork and began stuffing hay through the window.

Lufkin was unconscious, and Hondo hoped he would stay that way. He saw Rumel Thornberry light a cigarette as he waited in the stable door. He leaned the pitchfork up against the stable along with Gillette's rifle, and climbed through the hay window.

" No use bein' in a hurry to sling grain sacks," Rumel laughed. " Let them boogars sweat."

Hondo grunted something in reply, as he advanced in the dark. He knew that he was faintly visible, and since he was tall, and Lafe Lufkin was small he would be recognized instantly if Thornberry gave him a close look.

He suddenly thrust the barrel of his sixgun deep into Thornberry's stomach. " Make a sound and I'll blow your guts out," he hissed venomously.

Rumel gasped, and the cigarette in his hand described a swift arc downward.

" Hondo Horn ! " the fellow burst out involuntarily, with perhaps a bit of superstitious fear in his voice.

" Get 'em up, and keep shut," Hondo whispered viciously.

The man's hands started up, the right one still holding the cigarette. But suddenly he jabbed the lighted end of the cigarette straight into Hondo's face, struck viciously at the gun pressed against his stomach with the other, and twisted his lean body swiftly sideways.

Hondo fell back with an involuntary oath as the hot end

of the fag stuck against his cheek, but his thumb slipped off the cocked hammer of his gun, the slug just missing Rumel's body.

Rumel leaped over the door sill, grabbed frantically at his sixgun. Ignoring the pain in his face Hondo managed to grab his enemy's arm. They wrestled desperately for a moment, then Hondo caught his foe a glancing blow on the head with his gun barrel. It was hard enough to bring Rumel to his knees.

Rumel's hat fell from his head, and Hondo struck once more; this time with all the power in his arm. Rumel Thornberry fell prostrate.

That shot blasting out of the stable was like a bombshell tossed among the men who had congregated where Ez Thornberry had stopped his wagon directly under the unloading platform of the granary.

Ez had just lifted his tall, gaunt form up on the platform to receive and empty the sacks as the other men handed them up to him. All unknowingly he presented a magnificent target from the open-sided blacksmith shop.

" Look out, men ! " he bellowed entirely too late. " Git—"

He was cut short by a bullet that smashed through his breast bone. He turned half round, then fell crashing to the ground in the narrow space between the wagon and the granary.

" Come on, Hondo," Pat Young yelled. " Give 'em hell ! "

Chapter XXIV The Day of Damnation

The five other men had taken refuge behind the loaded wagons. The teams were drawn up in a line. Ez Thornberry had tied his team, and one of the leaders of each successive team had been tied to the tail-gate of the wagon ahead.

It was a loose arrangement, and as the firing broke out the horses tried to get away. The wheelers crowded up on to the leaders, which were restrained by their tie-ropes. Some wheelers got their front feet into the stretcher-bars of the leaders and began to plunge. In a moment all was pandemonium, as horses plunged and fell, tangled themselves in the harness of other horses, and wagons cramped and overturned.

Meanwhile, the day of damnation seemed to have arrived. The five survivors were blazing away at anything they thought moved. One of Thornberry's pigs raced across the yard and instantly three streaks of orange flame leaped toward it. Hit, the animal fell on its hips, squealing as only a wounded pig can squeal, while it turned around on its tail, with its front legs still straight. Its frantic squeals of pain were contagious, and from the pig-pens all the other swine joined in the uproar.

It would have been suicide for Hondo to attempt to cross the yard. He raced around the end of the stable and got hold of Ace Gillette's carbine. Then, whenever he saw the flash of a gun from the wagons he let go with a bullet. From the blacksmith shop Pat Young kept up a steady, rat-tat-tat with his sixgun.

The careening wagons became too dangerous. Two of the men tried to reach the granary, the closest shelter at hand. Hondo fired three times at the legs of one man and brought him down. Another rammed his breast squarely against a bullet spewing from Pat Young's sixgun. The other three, however, ran for the house, and were well sheltered by the wagons.

Hondo took dead aim at the wounded pig. It fell on its side, and its hideous squeals ceased instantly.

"Come on," Pat yelled eagerly, "the skunks are gettin' away."

Hondo ran over to the shop, and ducked hastily inside as a bullet smacked into a board within a foot of his head.

"We can wipe 'em out," Pat yelled excitedly. "You pour it on 'em with that rifle, while I circle around below the house."

"Hey, wait! be careful, Pat!" Hondo called, but the excited Pat had already left his shelter. He was running fast and low, and there was nothing for Hondo to do except fire as rapidly as he could.

They had overlooked Ez Thornberry. The man was not dead—yet. As he saw Pat run past the granary he raised up with a final effort, and fired. The heavy slug struck Pat just back of his right ear. The ex-convict fell forward upon his face, dead almost as he struck the ground!

Hondo felt a wave of grief as he saw his friend fall. Pat had the great virtue of loyalty. He would never desert a friend. But Hondo realized instantly that Pat had died exactly as he would have wished. Had he lived he would have had to go back to the penitentiary, or lived on a brief while as a hunted fugitive.

Now Hondo was alone. He could tell by the streaks of powder flame that he still had three foes to deal with—and one man couldn't surround a house. He didn't know whether or not any of his foes had been killed, and he didn't care. What he wanted was a prisoner.

He continued to exchange shots with his foes at the house until the cartridges in the magazine of the carbine were exhausted. He had no more. He noticed that only two men were firing now; whether he had hit one, or what, he didn't know.

He abandoned the rifle and got back behind the stable. He was just in time to see Lafe Lufkin get to his feet, weaving drunkenly. The fellow turned as he heard Hondo, and reached uncertainly for his gun. Hondo was close enough to whack him across the knuckles this time, and Lufkin howled with pain.

"All right, firebug," Hondo said grimly, "you're going with me."

"Wh—where's Rumel?" Lufkin mumbled.

"Dead," Hondo replied ominously. "So is Ez—and the rest of 'em."

That seemed to bring the fellow to his senses. "What you gonna do with me?" he whined.

"Me? Scarcely anything," Hondo said.

With a sixgun at his back Lufkin marched reluctantly up to where the two horses waited. Hondo forced him to mount, and made sure that he stayed there by tying his ankles to the stirrups.

Leaving Pat Young lying down there dead was one of the hardest things Hondo had ever had to do, but his job wasn't half finished. It would be only a matter of hours until he had to surrender to the law, and in that brief time he had to clear his name, and that of the dead Willard Dixon as well, or face the certainty of an ignominious death on the scaffold.

It was strange how thoughts of Daphne kept running through his mind. She, probably, had forgotten all about him in her grief over her brother, but he wanted to make her the gift of proof that Willard's last confession was a lie.

With his now sullen prisoner Hondo cut back through the hills to a small canyon that ran out on the plain to strike Swan Creek midway between Swan Basin and the K Bar K. It was coming dawn, the ending of the most tumultuous night Hondo had ever passed. But, had he been a woman, he would have cried with vexation that it was so short. Being a man all he could do was swear. He had intended to make a lone-handed raid on Brig Dow's place, and make that candidate for sheriff a prisoner. Now it was too late. Grimly he held on his course toward the K Bar K.

Then, as he came in sight of the familiar ranch buildings, he saw a dozen men top a small ridge to the south. They were riding at a trot, but at sight of him and his prisoner they spurred up to a gallop.

"To hell with you," Hondo muttered, as he spurred his horse to a run, fairly dragging the animal Lufkin was on. All he wanted was to get Lafe Lufkin into the house and turn him over to the K Bar K boys. Once he told them that Lufkin was the firebug who had burned Bessie's buildings he believed they would extract a confession from the fellow if it was humanly possible.

It was thoroughly light now, although the sun wasn't yet above the hills. He saw old Bilious, the coloured cook, come out of the house and wave his arms wildly.

Hondo spurred still more frantically, wondering the while why the men who had fallen in behind him didn't shoot. They must know who he was, but he didn't look back until he galloped into the yard.

"Where's the boys, Bilious?" he demanded.

"A-comin' right behind yo', Mist' Hondo, fas' as dey kin git dey hosses to run," Bilious answered with a wide grin.

Hondo jerked his head around. It was true. It was the K Bar K crew, and the old man himself was in the lead. He waited for them to ride up.

"Hondo! What'n'ell are you doin' here?" George A. bellowed. "Where did you git that?"

"This is the pretty lad that set fire to Bessie Bell's livery and feed store last night," Hondo said. "I heard him bragging about it to Rumel Thornberry last night. I brought him here for you boys to work over until he decides to put it down in writing—with some other things."

"Burned? A fire! Was anybody hurt?" Kump inquired.

"I don't think so, but Ace Gillette is going to be awful mad when he finds out I didn't burn up in it, because I stole his horse."

"And here I've rode all night to overhaul these boys and take 'em back to town so you wouldn't be lynched," Kump sighed, as he got stiffly to the ground. "I ain't used to it any more. When was the fire?"

"Soon after you left town."

Kump scratched his head. "What I can't see is why they started that rumour you were down on Rock River. They told the boys here, too, and they lit a shuck right down there on the chance they could pick you up before the sheriff did."

"We're for you, Hondo, no damn matter what they say," Ben Rambeau stated.

"It was like the Thornberrys," Hondo said. "Without Slick Abel you could put all their brains inside a peanut shell, even Brig Dow's. They can't see over little things. They thought they saw an opportunity to steal back those oats we got away from them."

"You mean they were here last night—with wagons?" George A. blurted.

"Those look like wagon tracks to me," Hondo pointed out. "And I saw the wagons when they pulled in to Thornberry's."

They all missed the half deaf cook's weak, "I *thought* I heard somethin' once," as they pelted Hondo with questions as to what he was doing at Thornberrys'.

He quieted them, and gravely told them of the fight there, and of Pat Young's death.

They were silent for a moment after he finished.

"By Gawd, I say let's string Lafe Lufkin up to the boom-pole of the derrick, then go back and finish the rest of them," Spike Williams cried angrily.

"I'd rather get hold of Brig Dow," Hondo said. "I know he's been mixed up in all of it. I think he'd cave like a sand-bank if we told him Lufkin had confessed. But it's too late now, I guess."

"It may not be," Kump said. "Boys, lock Lufkin in the cellar, and get rid of those two horses. I think I can get a confession from Dow just by telling Judge Tillman that Lufkin has accused him of starting that fire. You better stay under cover, Hondo."

"No," Hondo refused quietly, "I'm seeing this thing through. I'll go to town with you."

The cowboys started to protest, but desisted when they noticed that their employer did not join them. Then they demanded the privilege of accompanying them, but this, too, was denied. "You just go on about your business. Because you rode all night you don't need to leave the place. If anybody inquires about Lufkin you don't know anything about him."

"Can't we work on him a bit?" Spike pleaded. "I know several good ways to make a man talk."

Lafe Lufkin had listened to all this conversation. He looked hollow-eyed and frightened. Surrounded by men of his own kind he was brave enough. But here he was alone—surrounded by enemies. He glanced anxiously at George A. Kump's homely face. What words came from those thick lips might easily decide his whole future life—if any.

"H-m," George A. murmured. "No, just let him think it over in peace and quiet. Maybe he'll decide he'd better talk than be tied up for the rats to nibble his toes."

It was a reprieve, but far from comforting. The men dragged him from his horse and down to the cellar underneath the old ranch-house.

"I don't advise you going to town, Hondo," George A. said gravely. "Feeling is pretty high, and so far we haven't got a thing."

"Except one thing," Hondo corrected. "We've got Slick Abel's blunder."

"Yeah, we have, and it's something I never would have thought of myself," George A. admitted. "But it's a slender thread to hang your life on."

"Let's go," Hondo said.

Chapter XXV — "Hold Everything"

Daphne was the first to discover the fire. An excited yell in the street sent her flying to the window. She saw the fire in the front end of the livery stable, and screamed at Bessie.

Bareheaded, the two girls raced over to join the rapidly growing but helpless crowd.

"Hondo is in there," Daphne whispered. "Do you think he can get out?"

"Of course he will," Bessie said without conviction. "Don't get too close. I'm going around back. Maybe they can save the horses."

Daphne followed close at Bessie's heels. Someone tried to stop them.

"Get out of my way," Bessie said angrily. "This is my property that's burning."

She could see that most of the horses were out, and several men were getting out more. Someone was yelling at them to stay clear, that the roof would fall in any minute. Once more they were stopped, this time forcibly. And suddenly they saw the front end of the roof collapse. It would be but a matter of minutes until the rest followed. The terrific heat from the burning hay and timbers drove everybody back.

"Hondo Horn was in there," they heard a man shout. "He dived right under that falling roof. I saw him!"

Daphne noticed Bessie just in time to catch the older woman as she fainted. She felt like fainting herself, but it would never do. She had just lost her brother, but, somehow, this was an even worse blow. She didn't know how she could have changed from hating this man so bitterly, to feeling such tremendous grief at his death.

Somebody brought a hatful of water and dashed it in Bessie's face. It was Hank. Bessie sat up with a start. Between them Daphne and Hank got her farther from the fire. It was plain by then that both buildings were doomed.

"Did you see Hondo, Hank?" Bessie inquired.

"Yeah, it was him who raised the alarm. He got most of the horses out. They say he must have set the fire, but he come out of the feed store, and the fire started in the loft. I didn't dare say anything, o' course."

"No, of course not. Are—are you sure he's dead, Hank?"

"I seen him divin' back toward the harness room just as the roof fell."

"I can't stand it," Bessie moaned. "Take me home, Hank."

Daphne went with them to the street, and stopped. Bessie was mourning Hondo as her own dead, and Daphne felt that her presence was an intrusion. And now, somehow, she didn't believe that Hondo was dead, in spite of seemingly irrefutable evidence. She had the feeling that if he was dead she would know it.

She stayed to watch the buildings burn to the ground, keeping well away from the crowd, which finally began to disperse. She saw Ace Gillette and the night marshal standing together near the fire. They had been busy keeping the crowd back out of the danger zone. They hadn't noticed her at all.

Finally she heard Gillette say, "Well, Max, it looks like the excitement is all over. I'm not a damned bit sure about this fire. Why should it happen just when there was a false rumour about Hondo Horn?"

"You can search me," the marshal invited.

"I've had about enough," the young deputy said harshly. "But I guess I'll have to hunt up Watson and tell him Hondo is dead. Chances are I'll have to ride all night."

Daphne had been standing in the shadows of a shoemaker's small shop not far from the burned buildings, and the two officers were at the corner of the building. The marshal didn't go away, and she could not move without him seeing her. It would lead to questioning, and she didn't want to talk. So she waited. She had resolved to return to the hotel. Somehow she couldn't bear to solace Bessie in her grief over a man whom Daphne also loved.

The marshal started away, then came back. A man came galloping down the street on a barebacked horse. It proved to be Ace Gillette. He pulled up by the marshal.

"That damned Hondo didn't burn up," Gillette said angrily. "He got away and stole my best horse and saddle."

"Why, the ungrateful son-of-a-gun," the marshal said.

"Aw, hell, I'm glad he didn't burn to death, but it means another manhunt, and I suppose a few more murders," Gillette said. "I never thought Hondo would go wrong. Can I borrow your saddle?"

"Sure, help yourself."

The men moved off together, and Daphne was free at last to move. She ran swiftly across the street to Bessie's place and threw open the door. Bessie and Hank were before a fire in the grate. "I thought you must have gone back to the hotel," Bessie said without interest.

"No, I've been watching the fire," Daphne cried. "And I just found out—Hondo isn't dead."

"What?" Bessie exclaimed excitedly. "Are you sure?"

Daphne told them what she had heard, and her voice was vibrant and eager. Bessie's manifest relief gave way to a look of curious interest as she watched the girl's animated face.

"I hate to dash your jubilation, dearie," Bessie said at last, "but it might have been better for Hondo if he had burned up in that barn. It would be better than hanging."

"I don't believe it," Daphne cried. "He isn't guilty. I've known that ever since Willard told me the truth about him. We'll prove it someway. We've got to."

She would have returned to her hotel, but Bessie wouldn't hear of it. Instead, they sent the now homeless Hank over to the hotel.

"Thanks for telling me about Hondo getting away," Bessie

said, as they were preparing for bed. " I guess for a while I kind of let go. We can't afford to do it."

Daphne was up long before Bessie the next morning. There was nothing left of the two buildings across the street except smoking embers, but it was easier to breathe knowing that there wasn't a man's charred bones among the embers.

By the time Bessie got up the curious were already around viewing the heap of ashes. Whether they still believed Hondo Horn was under them or not Daphne didn't know.

They had scarcely finished breakfast when young Harold Thatcher called. Although he tried to maintain the frosty dignity of his office he was plainly embarrassed.

" I came to see Miss Dixon," he said, when Bessie finally got him seated.

" Yes ? " Daphne said, her heart turning over several times.

" First, I wish to express my sympathy about your brother, you know," he said awkwardly.

" Oh, sure," Bessie put in ironically.

" I admit that I've been almost overwhelmed by the wave of lawlessness that has swept over this country," Thatcher said. " It pains me very much, Miss Dixon, to have to tell you that a warrant for your arrest has been sworn out. You are accused of subornation of perjury and conspiracy. The complaining witness is one William Burgess who alleges that you paid him a thousand dollars to swear to a falsehood in court. Do you deny the allegation ? "

" Look here, Thatcher : is she on trial ? " Bessie demanded.

" Of course not. I only hope I'll not have to prosecute this case, but the evidence does seem uncontrovertible," the attorney bridled.

" It's all right, Bessie," Daphne said quietly. " I'm perfectly willing to answer the gentleman's questions, although if he believes my brother's alleged confession I don't suppose I can change his mind."

" You yourself have identified your brother's signature."

" But he swore to it because he thought I was being held prisoner by Rumel Thornberry, which I was for a time."

" That's hardly a valid reason for a man to swear his life away."

" You are aiding the real murderers," Daphne said.

Thatcher chose to ignore that. " I have the sworn statement of William Burgess that you gave him a thousand dollars to swear that he saw the man known as Hondo Horn give your brother a sum of money. I have a promissory note signed by you for five hundred dollars made out to Aaron Abel," he said. "Now the only reason I'm coming to you is this. There is no question in my mind that Horn did give your brother that money. Now it is no excuse in law for you to break the law to prove the point, but I think I can understand your feelings in the matter."

"I gave Burgess the thousand dollars. At the time I sincerely believed that he was telling the truth," Daphne declared.

Thatcher smiled wearily. "If it had been the truth it shouldn't have been necessary to pay him to swear to it," he stated.

"Just what did you come here for?" Bessie demanded.

"I came to urge Miss Dixon to plead guilty to a simple charge of subornation of perjury. I'm sure the court will consent to be lenient. I'm not unaware, Mrs. Bell, that Miss Dixon deliberately tried to defend Hondo Horn when he was accused of the murder of Ozark. She must have been an eye-witness to that, yet she has denied that Horn and Young committed that murder. If the case goes to trial all such things will work against the court's inclination to show mercy,' Thatcher argued.

Bessie strode over to the window. "All I can say is that you and Sheriff Watson make me sick. Thinking Hondo is guilty and working for the very people who are out to throw you out of your jobs."

"That is a matter," the prosecutor said with dignity, "which I do not choose to discuss. I am asking Miss Dixon to plead guilty. It will mean the difference between probably three or four years in the penitentiary, and a mere six months in jail."

Either prospect was horrible enough to make Daphne shudder. She realized that she not only had no money, she owed Slick Abel five hundred dollars. It was a temptation to plead guilty, even though she was innocent, and get the whole thing over with as quickly as possible.

"No," she said, after a brief hesitation, "I've committed no crime, and I won't say that I did."

Attorney Thatcher shrugged. "Then I have no——"

"Hold everything!" Bessie cried sharply. "My God! Look who's coming up the street. It's George A. Kump and —Hondo Horn!"

CHAPTER XXVI HONDO GOES ON TRIAL

DAPHNE beat Harold Thatcher to the window by a stride. She gave a glad cry that caused Bessie to whirl and look at her.

"I—I—can't believe it," the bespectacled young attorney muttered. "The—the sheriff should be here."

Daphne beat both her companions to the door. The two men immediately rode up to Bessie's picket fence.

"I say," Thatcher muttered at Hondo, "are you under arrest?"

"I was, unless I've been acquitted," Hondo replied serenely. "Wasn't this the day set for my preliminary hearing?"

"Why—why, yes, I think so."

"Well, the defence is ready to proceed," Hondo said.

"On your way, son," George A. addressed the prosecutor, but wild horses couldn't have dragged young Thatcher away.

"I know you're not guilty, Hondo," Daphne said. She was beside his horse, she wanted to touch him, but she only stroked his horse's mane. Then his hand came down over hers.

"It's all right, honey," he said. "There's been some trouble, but we've got a confession now that clears up the whole thing."

"A confession?" Thatcher asked eagerly.

"At the proper time," George A. said with dignity, "we shall prove not only that Willard Dixon was framed for the murder of Tim Bell, but that his alleged confession was secured by duress because he believed his sister's life would be forfeited if he refused. We'll prove who murdered Tim Bell, Ozark, Gus Marks, and Willard Dixon. And Hondo and Willard are as innocent as you are."

"I hope so," said Thatcher weakly.

A number of men had emerged from the Senate Saloon. Among them were Brig Dow, Slick Abel, and Heb Giles. All of them acted as if they were sitting on an ant hill.

"I think your friends up there want to see you, Thatcher," Hondo said, "but I can break the news. The Thornberrys tried to steal six wagon loads of oats from the K Bar K last night. When me and Pat Young tried to stop 'em there was some trouble. Pat was killed."

For a moment Hondo's voice broke. Then he went on, " I don't know whether anybody else got it or not, but some of 'em were shot. And as soon as my hearing is over I want Rumel Thornberry arrested for the murder of Ozark."

" And Brig Dow for the murder of Willard Dixon," Kump put in.

Unable to get any more details from them Thatcher started toward the courthouse, but stopped when he was hailed by Attorney Abel. Dow and Giles hurried over with Abel to question the young prosecuting attorney. He talked with them a minute or so, then resumed his way. Abel and the others hurried back to the saloon, where a crowd was rapidly collecting.

" You fellows can't fool me," Bessie said crisply. " You're bluffing."

" God help us, we are, but it's the only chance we've got," George A. said.

Daphne clung to Hondo's hand, and kept her eyes fixed upon his face. She had for the moment forgotten all about Bessie's prior claim.

" I've been arrested, too," she said in a small voice.

" I think you'll be safe," Hondo smiled.

" Anyway, if you've been arrested I'll go see about arranging bail," George A. said.

Daphne remembered that this homely old man had lost ten thousand dollars putting up bail for her brother.

" I can't let you do that," she said. " I'm willing to go to jail."

" Not if I can help it," George A. growled. He turned to Bessie. " Them buildings were fully insured, wasn't they ? "

Bessie nodded.

Hondo and George A. rode on to the courthouse, with Bessie and Daphne following along like two children.

Perhaps an hour later Sheriff Watson rode into town accompanied by his chief deputy and his posse. All were weary and bad tempered. Dr. Beck and several other men had gone out to Thornberry's ranch, but they had not yet returned.

Heb Giles, however, was in town, and he had been one of the men at the fight. According to Giles, Ezra Thornberry, Dutchie, and Pat Young were dead. Rumel Thornberry had a cracked skull. Johnny Jebbs had been shot in the leg, and Lafe Lufkin had disappeared utterly.

Walk Thurgood, and one of Brig Dow's hired men named

Chris Cratt, had remained at the Thornberry place to care for the wounded while Giles had gone to Dow's ranch, whence he and Dow had hurried to town with the story of bloodthirsty crime and slaughter upon the part of the already bloody-handed Hondo Horn. Their amazement at seeing Horn himself ride up the street with an air of supreme confidence had been no little. Nor had the things the young prosecuting attorney relayed to them served to bolster their morale.

It was soon all over town that Hondo Horn was in the courthouse and that his preliminary hearing for the murder of Ozark was about to begin.

Slick Abel, too, was at the courthouse, arguing angrily with young Thatcher and Judge Tillman that the hearing should be delayed until a full report was made on the last killings.

Judge Tillman, a small, wiry old man of sixty, was adamant.

"This case will go on," he declared firmly. "The prosecution is ready, the defence is ready, and the court is ready. One would almost suppose, Mr. Abel, that you did not want the accused to stand trial on this count."

Abel's bald head turned crimson. "The defendant is not represented by counsel," he said weakly.

"The defendant chooses to represent himself," the judge said.

Hondo Horn sat at a table with George A. Kump, Daphne, and Bessie. The courtroom was jammed. Hondo had worn his sixgun into the room, but had at once stuck the weapon in a drawer of a table provided for the defence. Perhaps not half a dozen people saw him do it. The rest, noticing his empty holster, assumed that he had been disarmed.

Ace Gillette was the first witness called by Thatcher. He told of meeting Hondo Horn, and of finding Ozark's body at the Thornberry place. He then went on to tell what the Thornberrys had said about the way Hondo Horn had brought the body there, and what he had said.

"That is not a proper line of questioning," Judge Tillman told Hondo. "I'll sustain an objection."

"I don't want to object," Hondo said. "Let him talk."

Gillette stared thoughtfully down at Hondo.

"I'll not pursue that line of questioning further, your Honour," Thatcher said. "I'll ask the witness one more question. Mr. Gillette, was the dead man, Ozark, wearing an undershirt?"

" He was," Ace answered.

" Describe the condition of that undershirt, please."

" It was covered with blood and powder burns."

" Is this the shirt ? " Thatcher demanded.

" I'll say that it is."

" You identify it positively ? "

" I do."

" Your Honour, the prosecution offers this shirt in evidence as Exhibit A. That is all."

" Just a minute," Hondo said, as the deputy started to step down. " Are you familiar with powder burns ? "

" I think I am," Ace answered belligerently.

" You are sure then that the powder burns on this shirt were made before any blood seeped through it ? " Hondo asked quietly.

The courtroom tensed. Ace Gillette looked worried. " Lemme see that shirt again," he requested.

" I object," Hondo said in a suddenly steely voice. He was on his feet in front of the deputy.

" Sustained," grinned the judge.

" You had plenty of opportunities to see that undershirt. If I shot Ozark from a distance so close as to leave powder marks they would only show where the shirt was not soaked with blood. Isn't that true ? "

Young Thatcher was too interested to object.

" Yeah, that would be true," Gillette admitted.

" Then do you want to swear on your oath that you know the powder burns were made before the bleeding started ? " Hondo demanded.

" No, I can't," the deputy stammered. " I—I just assumed they were."

Judge Tillman leaned over his desk. " Are you contending, Hondo, that the powder burns were made after Ozark was murdered ? " he asked with amazement.

" I am," Hondo said. " Examine that shirt under the microscope, your Honour, and you can see that the powder burns were made *hours* after Ozark was dead."

" Do you claim to have evidence that someone deliberately discharged a gun against this shirt while it was on the dead body of the man Ozark ? " Judge Tillman asked.

Hondo turned to face the court. " Your Honour, I wouldn't have come in here and give myself up if I hadn't had that proof. I ask for a recess of one hour. At that time I'll produce Lafe Lufkin, who will swear that the powder burns on this undershirt were made at the Thornberry ranch, and the gun containing the blank cartridges was held by Slick Abel."

"That's a lie!" Abel shrieked.

"Why, that ain't anything to what we will prove on you, Slick," Hondo said casually. "For one thing you'll hang for the murder of Gus Marks."

"Your Honour, I appeal——" Abel yelled wildly.

"If you have such proof, Hondo, why aren't your witnesses here in court?" the judge demanded.

"Because it was necessary to confront Rumel Thornberry and two or three other guilty persons with Lafe Lufkin before Slick Abel and Brig Dow, who are more guilty, could get hold of them," Hondo said easily.

It was the biggest bluff of his life. Nobody had even tried to make Rumel Thornberry or anyone at his place confess. But it was known that Lufkin was missing. Slick Abel and Brig Dow knew that, too. And it was upon the actions of these two men that Hondo was gambling his life. That, and the fact that Slick Abel had slipped up with the powder burned shirt.

Ace Gillette, who was still seated on the witness stand, suddenly yelled, "Come back here, Dow!"

The man who wanted to be sheriff plunged headlong into the crowd. An instant later Slick Abel fled the other way, toward Judge Tillman's chamber. As he did so he threw out his left arm and caught Daphne around the neck, forcing her back against his breast. He reached under his frock coat for a small six-shooter in a concealed holster, and his face was twisted into a gargoyle's mask of hate as he thrust the gun past the girl's body to fire at Hondo Horn.

Hondo leaped, and felt something slam into his chest like a sledge hammer, but it didn't stop him.

"Stay back, or I'll kill this girl!" Abel screamed, but he fired a second shot at Hondo.

Hondo felt his left arm go dead, but his right fist whizzed over the top of Daphne's head and struck Abel on the side of the nose, and the eye. The lawyer sprawled backward, dragging Daphne down with him.

There was a slogging pain in Hondo's breast. There was a wild ringing in his head that was not caused by the yelling crowd. By sheer power of will he retained consciousness. He knew but one thing. If he didn't grab that gun Slick Abel would kill Daphne with it.

He saw the barrel of the gun and lunged at it. He fell on his side, across the tangled legs of Abel and Daphne, but his good hand had the barrel of the gun. Through slitted eyelids he saw the look of crazed fear and murderous hatred on the lawyer's face. It was Hondo Horn Slick Abel wanted to kill. He got hold of the gun with both hands, and swung the weapon around until it almost pointed at Hondo's head.

Then, calling upon the last reserve of his strength and stamina Hondo suddenly doubled his foe's elbow back. The tightly gripped sixgun reversed direction, and its muzzle was thrust against Abel's throat. The weapon barked viciously, and blood spurted from the lawyer's jugular vein.

George A. Kump and Bessie pulled the tangled three apart. Daphne needed no help, but Hondo's strength was suddenly spent.

Brig Dow had been brought down before he could get halfway through the crowd. Ace Gillette presently got the man into the sheriff's office, and Sheriff Watson, Harold Thatcher, and even Judge Tillman quickly joined them. Dow cowered fearfully in a chair.

"You want to talk now, Dow, or will you wait for the Thornberrys to pin everything on you?" the sheriff growled.

"I'll talk," Dow said. "All I wanted was to be sheriff. Slick Abel said if we could throw you people out of office there would be rich pickings. He said all we needed to do was discredit Hondo Horn and the K Bar K to make it a cinch."

"But you knew all about these killings," Judge Tillman charged.

"And you killed the Dixon boy," the sheriff said.

"No, I didn't," Dow denied vehemently. "I didn't kill nobody. It was Rumel Thornberry killed the Dixon kid. I took the credit because they said it would help my campaign."

"You know who killed Tim Bell, don't you?" Watson asked.

"It was Ozark. That started the whole thing. Slick Abel said we could use the frame-up on the Dixon kid to frame Hondo Horn. When Kump stood by him that was all we wanted," Dow said.

"And one killing led to another," Judge Tillman cried angrily. "Who killed Ozark?"

"That was Rumel, too."

"Who killed Gus Marks?" the sheriff demanded.

"That was Slick Abel. He went out there to see the Thornberry boys, and finding Gus Marks tied up he killed him so Hondo would be blamed. But Hondo Horn or Pat Young killed Ez Thornberry and Dutchie," Dow declared.

"If they did it was justified," the judge barked. "We'll say it was Pat Young anyway."

While the examination was going on the bespectacled young prosecuting attorney had fidgeted nervously, unable to get in a word. Now he finally made himself heard.

"What do you know about the Bill Burgess business?" he asked Dow.

"I don't know nothing," the man said sullenly, "except that Slick Abel framed the whole thing to get the Dixon girl where he wanted her."

"You mean he advised her to pay Burgess the thousand dollars?"

"Of course. She thought Burgess had seen Hondo give her brother the money, and Slick made her think it was the only way she could get him to testify."

Brig Dow had no more than been locked in his cell when Dr. Beck and the party that had gone out to Thornberry's returned. They confirmed what Heb Giles had said about the results of the battle. They said the wagons were still loaded with grain, but nothing had been seen of Lafe Lufkin.

That mystery was not solved until George A. Kump was called in.

Once more the old cowman-banker was the most influential citizen of his county. The officers listened with deference while he told them of Hondo's colossal bluff.

"Hondo simply gambled his life that Abel or Dow would crack when he sprang it on them that Lufkin had confessed, but I doubt if they would have done it had not Slick made that mistake about the powder burns. If Slick had known as much about guns as he did about law he wouldn't have pulled that one," George A. smiled.

"You mean to say that Lufkin *didn't* confess?" Judge Tillman demanded. "I think somebody ought to be fined for contempt of court for taking me in that way."

"He hasn't confessed yet, but when he finds out that Brig Dow had, and that Slick Abel has killed himself I have no doubt he will," George A. said placidly.

He was a true prophet. When Rumel Thornberry was tried for murder six weeks later it was Lufkin's testimony, even more than Brig Dow's, which convicted him.

Rumel Thornberry was sentenced to hang for the murder of Ozark. Brig Dow received twenty years in the penitentiary, and Lafe Lufkin ten. Other members of the gang with which Slick Abel had hoped to loot the county received from one to five years.

Hondo Horn got out of bed to testify at Rumel Thornberry's trial. When it was over and he was back in his room at Nick Cropopolos' hotel Bessie came to see him.

"I dropped in to say good-bye, Hondo," she smiled. "I'm leaving Highline."

"You're leaving? Good grief, why?" he blurted.

"Well, I've collected my insurance, and George A. has bought my house. I've got plenty of money, and I want to see the world," she said brightly.

"We've been pretty honest with each other, Bessie," he said. "You know how I feel about you. I think you're the squarest guy in the world."

"I know." She turned away to dab furtively at a stray tear. "I think you're pretty grand yourself. I may envy Daphne at times, but that'll be because George A. told me, in strict secrecy, of course, that he was going to make you and her his heirs. She's a good kid, Hondo, and she loves you."

There was nothing Hondo could say. Bessie kissed him.

"She's downstairs listening to Nick," she said. "I'll send her up."

Daphne knocked timidly a few minutes later.

"Come in," Hondo called.

"Do—do you feel all right?" she asked. "After the excitement of the trial—and all."

"I feel fine," he said.

They looked into each other's eyes a moment, then his arms opened, and Daphne came into them. Hondo held his face pressed against her hair.

"I've loved you ever since Willard showed me your photograph," he said softly.

Daphne raised her lips to be kissed.

THE END